MW00415689

Shamp
of the
City-Solo
A NOVEL
BY Jaimy Gordon

*With drawings by James Aitchison
and an afterword by the author*

McPherson & Company

Shamp of the City-Solo

for Larry Eldredge

Copyright © 1974, 1980, 1993 by Jaimy Gordon.
Drawings copyright © 1974, 1993 by James Aitchison.
All rights reserved.

This edition first published in December 1993 by McPherson &
Company, Post Office Box 1126, Kingston, New York 12401. Publi-
cation has been assisted with grants from the literature programs
of the New York State Council on the Arts and the National
Endowment for the Arts, a federal agency. Manufactured in the
United States of America. Third Edition.
1 3 5 7 9 10 8 6 4 2   1993 1994 1995 1996

Library of Congress Cataloging-in-Publication Data

Gordon, Jaimy, 1944-
  Shamp of the city-solo
    p.   cm.
  ISBN 0-929701-34-8 (pbk.)
    I. Title
  PZ4.G6634Sh   1980   PS3557.0668
  813'.54   79-2479

Printed on pH neutral paper.

C O N T E N T S

Shamp
of the
City-Solo

Thanks All Around

From Shipoff I learned to move in the world: how to solo, to fit where your foot falls, and always to keep an eye on the exit; where you cannot rule, to serve; and to talk unceasingly, for no word is wasted, nor can a word be empty, but even popped off in vain, lights up the point that popped in the lector's brain.

He taught me to covet the life of a lector, to crave to orate the most timely topos from a lectern in Big Yolk, the city-solo. And when I was sixteen, and felled by my old foe Brakeknot along with the graveyard horse chestnut tree, I went with Shipoff.

A sample of our conversation:

Honored Shipoff! would I mind fetching you a beer?
Hughby, starboy! it's your pleasure.

And later in his Manuals:

When all else flops, one has yet to feed the starboy to the audience, done up grand, sure, but to go a long way...

Now observe, Shipoff knew what he did. Only look at his themesong:

O I was a Grecian braggadocio
The eyes a trope oer the level veldt
As I lengthened & strengthened so my head sweldt
But I towed the line and made it mind

1

Now tell me, wouldn't you like a little loving

O I was a Grecian braggadocio
A sabertooth in my semaphore
I stalked the stoutest youths before
They all went stale in the tailspin

Now tell me, &c.

Whatever he was, it came out of a coil. He left to the world the Shipovian Calculus, in which the Recoil is the move, yea, the master tropos of life—how to pass up nothing, but maintain the reversibility of your position at every turn. When faced with resistance he knew how to shrug, and suddenly make visible those coils to aft, streaming over his shoulder and all to the rear.

A practised picker and sorter of young men! may his bones find no receptacle. For his luck ran out, the track rolled around to where he set off on it, and I was on hand to see him come all ease around that bend so disarmingly like the others, to die still coming, a snake in his undoing.

To Tapsvine the World-Friar I owe my religious development, an eruption, it is true, he did all in his power to waylay. To Tapsvine I owe as well the normal state of my ears, the which, earnest lector, were not always so shapely as now. And he it was palmed me off on St. Cornwallis, after he had heard out my 21-point Waste Confession in the Depot chapel-loft, patiently smoking one pink and gold Suez fag after the other, hoping in vain to keep me out of his confessional for the rest of that week, blabbing, welching, and intra-community homicide notwithstanding.

And to the third of my worldly masters, Dr. Analarge, I owe the inspiration to dismiss all these other gifts out of hand, and to retire, in season, to my inexpressible side, the point where I, old Hughby, myself, Shamp, derail from the tracks of convention, now that my education at the hands, or was it the feet, of my worldly masters is complete. I owe more to the doctor, for that he would have kissed the instep, tears in his eyes, of a bitch like his daughter Yanneleh makes it kinder to believe that I cherished a stiff (Brakeknot) in my day over my own kind. But why deny it, I loved my masters too, each likewise in his day, although from that same Yanneleh, Annie Analarge, I received a sure cure against amatory passion—yea, hanging all night in the cold blow from the chapel gutter window had it all over her company.

And for getting me by all that I thank Providence...

And from Brakeknot, the primal master, ditto the foe? I learned the pleasures, most abominated of St. Cornwallis, of non-negotiability, home-hole, "pig-exile." To him is owed the simplicity of my tastes—never again an honest roof over my head, I go down the hole or, seasonably, up to my little twig shack—between green leaves, tracks of white sun. A few aspens to tell the time of year—a view of the new hotel that succeeded the Topical Tropists on the Depot dump—Shipoff, Analarge, Tapsvine, lectors, starboys, Annie, AUNTY, Grizzard, all.

O I have made regular blunders in my time. Scratching where I scratch, my health disorganized, my mind in decline, I rerun my bygone exit cringe by cringe, for want of cheaper entertainment. But after this parting gasp, earnest lector, I am never again to talk, blab, burble, twitter, twaddle, blubber, quibble, chatter, that much at least is behindhand, finished, kaput, for how much truth can a man afford to tell, if no word is wasted, and whatever he tells is truly told.

Granted that the same Shamp that speaks being Hughbury Shamp, the lector hand-torched for stardom in the city-solo with never an afternoon off without a kick in the tochos—granted he still sprouts his downy headbeams at the thought of a lit-up lectern. Only now, whereas once I would pace up and down the Sumpsky Prospect to make room for them, I now apply hair oil, and take them to bed.

As for the rest of my brother novices under Shipoff, the last of the Topical Tropists wheeled out of noseshot, waving, how-ever, towards their little stardoms in pulpits, tabloids, private

---

3

hibernacula, you name it. Or was it I that went? No. This is the terminal of all my promise. In this point all points east are sunk. Do I suffer, earnest lector?

I suffer? No I don't suffer. I'm just doing my rote ditty, I say, on the way out. And who does suffer? How long can he suffer, hovering over his severed parts, the curator of his pricks? What is it to lose it all, when that which a man has not, how can it hurt him? So I think back to St. Cornwallis, the fifes at Yorktown vitrifying that mortal starlight of day: *The World Turned Upside Down*. To old Cornwallis I owe—nothing, nothing, no more, by Chrust, than he owes me. Cornwallis at Yorktown, hearing that tune! The luxury of his loss, earnest lector! The grandeur, the totality of his disrepair.

I

Brakeknot

At seventeen, as yet unimproved by a master, I used to slink down the backstreets of Bulimy taking pains, with regard to my boyhood chums, to avoid crowds of three and more, as well as clumps of two or under, picking my way with a sort of eyeless joy through the railroad dump, hands pressed in pocket holes, pockets worn away, cutting across backyards, thence to the graveyard. The graveyard was the only unimproved parcel in town without a baseball diamond. Naturally, that's where I hung around.

Before my three worldly masters was Brakeknot. His stone leaned towards the street at a rakish angle, under a great horse chestnut tree half split at the crotch from old age and blight, but all the same deep in leaf.

> SGT. WEATHERALL BRAKEKNOT
> — June 8th 1908 —
> His Brother Optimists
> To His Memory
> Bulimy Co. Chapter
> Sgt.-At-Arms 1906 • 1908
>
> *At His Charge*
>
> 'Dede as a doornayle
> Doun was he fallen'
>
> Universally Esteemed
> And Regretted
>
> In the 55th Year
> Of His Age
>
> REST?

(The interrogative closer where a plain imperative is the custom would seem downright prophetic, had I not put it there myself, with a homemade awl, in an afternoon of tedious scraping.)

Sergeant Brakeknot: a lifelong bachelor, for only unmarried bones revert to the Bulimy County Optimists Society.

And although particulars are omitted, it's plain that some Optimist's mishap dispatched the Sergeant in his late prime, thereby depriving me of the pleasure. As for the specific cause, any native of Bulimy County knows that the second Sunday in June has been time out of mind the day of the Bulimy County Optimists' Annual Sing. Therefore if Brakeknot fell *At His Charge* on June 8 in any year, it could only have been at the Sing or at a rehearsal thereof.

What is more, the place of the Sergeant-at-Arms at every upcountry bash of this kind was not to sing. It was to present the colors with face of stone at the top of the quavering glee club, which at the Bulimy County Parade Ground would have placed Sgt. Brakeknot at one worm-eaten end or the other of the topmost plank of the most hazardous bleacher in seventeen counties, a State Farm reject without bench or railing. And so, had he been an average man, we would know that on June 8, whatever year, he departed this world by a fall off the festival grandstand, backwards.

He was anything but average, old Brakeknot.

Suppose as I supposed: that the Sergeant-at-Arms had a mark—a gift—a voice—a natural basso whose power had gained him a name in Bulimy at large, so that the Optimists could hardly pass up sending him on as a star. The Sergeant is called down from his plank, stripped of his flag, and pressed to lead one rare old favorite after another, in the key of his choice, for the ten-hour stretch.

Think of the sun and the crowd! Imagine a massive country basso, suffusing the canyon of bleachers and stands with a cloud of crapaudian diapasons. There is the Brakeknot—universally esteemed and regretted—who did not fall, but rather sang himself, to moral expiration.

A complete romantic, Brakeknot. From the start, fame was our common interest, and the way to fame was mastery of the situation. "Mastery by the voice, *naturellement!*" said the Sergeant. We agreed on everything. How was it we first began to take potshots at each other?

"By the voice—that peculiarly human extension—in speech! sneer! song! whatever the quarter hour requires."

I said that without a little renown for me at the center, life would seem to me a mistake, and consciousness just as well visited on a telephone booth or a railroad tie as on me. "Bravo!" cried the Sergeant, down the line. How was it we came up cross-eyed and pissing at each other?

If he was handicapped by great age and a lot of road wear, not to say an extinct condition, still Brakeknot took an edge in these discussions: he had his little fame already behind him. Still he resisted the facile sneers at fame that big city stars, already safely frozen beyond the stratosphere, like to have quoted under their names in the Big Yolk papers. Propaganda! Fashion! Bones to revolving Providence at best. I railed to the Sergeant that these familiar old tracks would never carry away the young rival rising out of the cowpie-cratered hills of Bulimy —namely myself, Shamp. Brakeknot said it was this sort of line that betrayed the formidable bastard I myself would be in my day of fame, if I didn't fizzle out first in a welter of persecution complexes.

When did we start swinging? Truly we discoursed like natural born gentlemen-soloists till he tracked down that hole in my presentation and, why deny it, started winning.

He struck me smack in a recoil, in a manner which Shipoff would have admired.

First off, he pretended to think I should play with other boys

—in truth his jaw always swung as from a meathook at my first step toward the street gate. I think that he loved me! Nevertheless he took this tack:

"There's a sinker in a match like ours," he would say, "that took off on the back of some weird hybrid between my rebirth and your, er, mortification." O, he did not mind, but it was not giving the young dogbait (the writer) an even break. "Granted your unwholesomeness is your own business, Hughby, I shrink from becoming its accomplice."

"Too bad that shrinkage doesn't push you beyond the bounds of visibility to the naked eye," I said. "It would be kinder to your pals."

"Maybe so, maybe so, but I might not get back. A reversible stance is one of the first measures of self-mastery! I'd rather be a little esteemed and a little regretted than universally regretted and never seen no more…"

"It must be fine to have a choice."

"And why not!" His bony old fingers made two tepees on the tombstone lectern. "Granted, to see a kid like you, young enough to make me choke, *rach-acheh-e-e-e-e!*"—(a little choke)—"is a nice twist in the always-the-same for an old dog like me. But it would be selfish of me not to point out that this is not the world, this here, nor even a respectable sampler…

"Now why don't you run play with your fellows?"

"But you've been off the street so long," I said. "It's not the world you'd like to think it is."

"Maybe not, my boy, if you're in it."

"It has its points! Number one: you're out of it."

"So why hang around?" he snarled. "My obsolescence was a matter of chronology. But yours, my boy, is a question of hygiene. What do you see in dead people?"

"Maybe I should be an Optimist?—you blew in and out of date like the English fart."

"You're a sarcophagus of obscenities!"

"You're an orchestra of senilities!"

Then I froze. For up to here I held my own, but just before

8

finishing me off the Sergeant would mesmerize me with the back of his head, yellow as a baseball under slate-green tendrils. Then, *hunh!* he whizzed full face, a thumb in each ear, wiggling his fingers and snorting cross-eyed:

"Upon my headstone, can't the boy ever talk, words enough to cause a good man to choke *(rach-acheh-e-e-e!)*—but Hughby, what do you know? Where were you when? Define yourself fifteen minutes ago!"

I shrugged.

"Names and faces!" he sneered. "A nobody! A likely story!"

"How about yourself? I suppose you call that old compost heap of morgue and barroom sweepings a somebody."

"No more, no less"—now he leaned forward till his nose point met mine—"but what I was, my own boy! What I was! What I was!"

Exit! For the old crumbum knew when to take off, an art that escaped me until only yesterday.

✧ ✧ ✧

It was not long before Shipoff happened along. The Sergeant's margin was slim, but it was diuturnal. One Friday I came to the iron street gate and cried:

"I'm sick of you, Sergeant. This mania for winning and nothing but winning! It's tedious, pop. I'll take your advice and give up the graveyard." And I left, give or take a point. True, I rotated around the fence a few times a day, on the outside. But it was not till 2 p.m. Monday, after the last time Truant Officer Peltman had cruised by the gate on his daily rounds, that I looked on the Sergeant's face.

And then I saw him,

Quantum mutatus ab illo!

He was a solemn and, who knows, to look at him, a sorry man. At least he was a speechless man. For that quickly his rant had given way to a ripe and perfect silence, unilateral in terms. It was a sham, but who was I to pass it up? "Old dog," I began—

9

> old dog Brakeknot,
> universally resteamed and confettied,
> I piss on your ashes—
> may they steam and confetti your butt-end …

And so on. I performed this orgy dutifully, though without enthusiasm. I wasn't born on the first of last week—I knew this turn of fortune for indulgence merely. And Brakeknot could never confine his genius to manuring my ego for more than a week, so it was no tickle to pull off those stale atrocities under the waxy nose and complaisant leer of the enemy himself.

Just such a day, Shipoff dropped in. I was offending Brakeknot, the two of us wreathed in yawns, both nodding off at a classical smear that had no smack of the earnest that pollutes the confidence of the honest offender. Earnest? When Brakeknot would be on my head again in a week?—a prospect so humdrum, and so deadly, that it rendered me grateful for a little diversion, a little deadpan sparring at his stone between snores—which Shipoff mistook for omnipotence.

> May you wake to the tune of fleas
> in 13 rebellious colonies
> mobilizing on your perineum
>
> O scabrous crust …

All lies, earnest lector. Among other faults, the Sergeant was clean as the day he was buried—even the worms had split for greener junctions. As for his health, the scrap that survived for the purpose was only too sound: he was Always-The-Same, a Soloist and a Traveller.

Nevertheless,

> Why should the old coot
> quit cultivating contagions
> to castigate his own corruption?
>
> Does the fish remonstrate with his pectorals?
>
> The king with his littorals?

The quean with her clitorals?

What he is he is and I piss on—

(Here I wearily pulled out my prop)

—his 2-ounce cranium
and his bog of empty underdrawers
flapping in the breeze ...

A rip and a crash! The piss froze midstream, but as I fell, I heard singing:

O I was a Grecian braggadocio ...
Now tell me, wouldn't you like a little loving?

When the bough breaks the cretin will fall. When the chestnut split in two, Shipoff followed in season, landing on all sixes* in the advanced anthropoid manner.

On his face, I thought, was real respect.

"Starboy, I'd like to do something for you. But I see by the bulge of your otherwise prepossessing eyeballs that your mother has hustled you out of consorting with strangers. Worn-out stump that she is, what does she know? Jawbones! There's no one else worth talking to."

Now, a more misguided view of my mother's social legislation, hysterical purely on the incentive side, could hardly be imagined. But calling my mother a worn-out stump—I blinked. What a stroke! What second sight endowed him with this information?

---

* Shipoff had two legs, each of which terminated in a foot. Sixes refers to his toes, the sixth being a nerveless and boneless appendage at the outer margin of each phalanx, a deformity so common as to have almost the status of a birthmark. Throughout the early months of our acquaintance, Shipoff not only waked and slept with his shoes on, but also made me take oath to insure, in the event of his death, that they were not removed before he was safely buried. Need I tell you that had he croaked I would have been the first one prying them off? However at the dawn of his success as leading lectromagnate of Big Yolk and the Americas, Shipoff suddenly ceased to conceal this affliction, and in fact ordered and wore custom-made cordovans with an eyelet at each outer sole, through which a sixth toe, fat and idle, might not only protrude but actually flop around in the public eye.

But perhaps I should have risen from the occasion with a trumped-up sang froid. All scruples of style aside, earnest lector, I was down for good reason—the foundered chestnut had laid me out, and lay in full if pimply leaf on the bias across my abdomen.

What is more, granted that of life the time is a point, it's a point at some junctures more accommodating than others. Is it stretching the point to say that at times the future lies on the present in plain sight, the present spreading for this with lamblike bleats? Who is surprised when it comes off the present a come (not a coming) thing, and what was the present is fucked! shucked! It's a new day.

"So you want to be a star in the city-solo!"

Although it was warm, the master sported two suits and four sport jackets, plus the canyons of esoteric bulges these layers deployed to his surface, three layers of long johns peeping out of his ankles and cuffs in descending scales of laundromatic yellow, a longcoat and a raincoat and a hogshead of neckties streaming out of his pockets, all of which gave him the air of a man who is going places, and as quickly as possible.

But I was staked to the ground by the tree like a hornworm to the drying board—what had I lost? It was hard to round it up...

It was Shipoff's pleasure to pack the lesion of self-possession with the lard of romance. Time will show it was owing to no deficiency in tactic that he picked this old home remedy out of his coils. There were bribes, browbeatings, bull-roarings in his train that might have done as well, and given a little novelty to the proceedings. But let us call to mind the ignorant native that the lectromagnate desired to bind to his administering thighbone as it trudged towards Big Yolk—

For I had never heard of a lector! And he rightly saw that the time was ripe to dole me an education.

First he inquired, fussing offhandedly in my foliage: "Do you always rage alone?"

Close to home! "I confess that I do," I lied.

"Hum. Disarming fweets and rolls. I am stopped by the way you fix a topos, going: the occasional curdler, tasteful. A 'primitive' lector type T (tirader) of fine points and to the tropos born, or my name ain't Leechin." It was Leechin, according to an Iznoczw Mohorovocic Free Library of Big Yolk borrower's card, expired, which he presently extended.

As he stared me very boldly in the eye, I stared back into his, for purposes of comparison. A disappointment: he had wino's eyes, the color of stroganoff.

"Now I'm no fool," he said, and ceasing to stare me in the eyes, he waded hand and foot in them. "Still I'm one of those fellows who live to adore—wipe the feet, pare the nails, trim the mustaches, tone up the fat of the beloved—even if I must, to

admire, and perish.

"I prefer to live of course! to pave the way to the fair for the beloved, to see his name in lights, timetables, trade digests, stock and farm reports…"

I was great with fame. Shipoff plumbed the branches and stuck his little hand into my fist. "Two bits to the corn-fed pork chop that pries you out of there. Then on to Big Yolk."

He let me carry his bag. "You don't have a quarter on you?" he said, giving his pockets the ritual frisk. The pork chop stood by patiently. I gave up a quarter. Shipoff explained: "My entire estate languishes in the Big Yolk P.O., pending my swift return."

It was the twelfth of October. I know for a fact that my disappearance never made the *Spirit of Bulimy-Longhorn Advocate*, because in one of the hours of confusion with which the next year was studded, I tried the Mohorovocic Free Library periodical file to find out.

Only under the Personals column the week after I left, I saw this thought-provoking item:

Is S. also among the prophets?

(—W.B.)

II

Luckenkamp

"Take his eyes!" said Shipoff. (*Viz.*, mine. By now he had got wind that the bulge was no flying buttress off the maternal conspiracy, but a private institution with a flatus all its own.)

"Take his eyes! Now, ten years to the rear of us, what a liability! And what would have been the only hope of the boy, with respect to his greater gifts, hanging as he was by an untrained lector's tonsile over the gorge of devouring obscurity? Nothing but the scalpel, cauteries, tongs, the gouge, lathe, dowel, etc., in a word, improving surgery. But not now. The age of the wholesale ectomy is out. It took its time going! Big Yolk is glutted with classic types. The stage is a hashery stew of them, you could puke for one more pretty face. Yes, the symmetrical bias is on the run. To hell with fashion, the females can't stand to look at each other.

"Now if even Hughby can have his day, and he will, never say that an honest-to-Chrust southern fried theo, er, fan like yourself, such as you don't see much anymore anyways, in especial one rolled in the froth of his rabid forefathers, salted with mother wit and peppered, above all, with a set of truly unusual facial characteristics (I'll venture to say unique)—that a face like your own stands in this day and age to get shunted back to the grade B chicken coop on the scruple of a 4-H mentality's idea of a taint, already ten years overdue in the grave. Well, I'll never believe it, not with what I know about Big Yolk. You listen to Shipoff. In the city-solo nowadays a rube arrives on what he's got, whatever, that the others haven't. Whatever! or let me spring a nose wen if I lie, or even if I don't lie, for a giant-size nose wen is money in the bank!

"Therefore"—for the closer, Shipoff plucked a chicken feather from the seatcover and picked his teeth with the quill—"it is my professional opinion that, like it or not, for better or worse, you will hit it big in Big Yolk as soon as you show that face on the sidewalk. Try singing a little. No, don't even try! They'll tear you apart. Well, better sing. Do something! Make the best of it. As long as you have that head your show is on the road, Chaspel Luckenkamp. Just roll into Big Yolk, and I Shipoff have said it."

Shipoff soon exhausted the chicken feathers at this rate, and applied his fingernails to the droppings, a thankless task in the best of henhouses. This, on the other hand, was a 1949 Dodge Wanderlust, a one-seater, its flesh-pink top trailing a home-made mobile poultry shed with unlimited passage, through the busted rear window, for a small fortune in Allegheny speckled leghorns.

As a vehicle, the Wanderlust had earthly imperfections in such measure as, were less than a thousand miles at hazard, might verily give even the lame to walk. But from Bulimy to Big Yolk was two thousand miles. And by now Shipoff's coils were hopelessly entangled in wringing out the immanent lift from here nonstop to the city-solo, with nightly chicken dinners, ours provided he could plant in the driver the conviction that his future too was lodged in the city-solo, complex, munificent and pent on his early arrival.

The driver's head had been the source and object of Shipoff's encouragements for two nights and a day now. It was a head so small that it fitted neatly into the rearview mirror, with both ears showing. For such a head Big Yolk was the only sanctuary, said Shipoff, or changing his tack he dwelt on the driver's chances in the rest of the world, which gave no quarter to freaks—the long shuffle between hounded obscurity and fugitive notoriety, dragging his chickens behind him.

Chaspel Luckenkamp, D.D., was the soul of attention. All the same he had doubts it was hard to part with, a hoarding gesture that did not confine itself even to the pardonable subject of his head. He had a tendency to look upon the dark side, long and lovingly, and to enlarge upon it without stint, that had crept upon him in the course of being run out of half the townships east of the Pecos, even though he bore the stickpin of the Grassroots Holiness Convention, and notwithstanding his corrective coiffure, which was just as interesting as the head which inspired it.

So at last he had invested his dwindling patrimony in chickens, and was driving around the country looking for a place to grow old in peace. Then he picked up Shipoff and me in the county of my nativity.

With that head, to pass up Big Yolk? The folly, the ignorant common selfishness, the contemptible self-abomination, Shipoff cried, of such a move.

"I have no doubt you speak the gospel as you see it," said Chaspel, "but being a Professor"—(this was a general expletive, on the order of Playboy or Politician)—"you can't appreciate how crowded my profession is. My field is so crowded!" His face, what there was of it, fell, or rather sank. "You don't know what it means—I don't even have a D.D.!"

"Eh-eh, brother doctor, we had the benefit of your introduction," said Shipoff. "Why worm out of it now?"

"All right! Honorary!—mailed from a Bible academy in Jamaica that had in mind, I believe, a touring chiropractor of like name, my distant cousin, deceased (by the grace of God) by the time I got him on the telephone."

Shipoff sniggered. "Just naturally kept it for yourself, eh? Got him on the telephone!"

"Aw shucks," Chaspel whined, his lip curdling over his uppers, "I needed it more than he did." He shot up recklessly to 25 miles per hour. "And anyway what is this grill job? Since

---

17

when do you have my best interests at heart? It wasn't for nothing I steered around Big Yolk for eight years on the Holiness circuit. The Reverend 'Sixfinger' Tweets of the Convention took me aside on a Blue Ridge Special, Big Yolk bound. He said, Steer clear of Big Yolk, that's the sideshow capital of the USA. Best you keep your head out of it, Chaspel, or you might wake up shanghaied to Steubenville, in a tent between a fat lady and a hootchee kootchee dancer. Yea, Big Yolk is a long drag on a short circuit, nor will the Glory Dinger up in heaven suffer it to repeat!"

The Glory Dinger at last. Yes, it was this flash of the Appointed in the corn pan of the renegade poultry farmer that alerted Shipoff he was making inroads. To little children a ball is a fine thing. He pursued this foul fly from Gopher Landing, Bulimy, to the Sumpsky Prospect, but we were in main smell of Big Yolk before Chaspel pleased to own up.

On the issue of his head, his heart was at ease. He confessed it was an asset, from Muncie at least. And surely that last lap from Muncie to the city-solo was more than he required for a competent anticlimax, low muttering variety, or any other variety. But Chaspel tortured Shipoff all the way with a delirium rote, cyclic, and foxily inquisitive between half-hour cycles, feverishly reiterating his second-string household anxieties until Shipoff took up making little puking noises for my private entertainment, and began eyeing my late daddy's railroad Longines, for nobody's entertainment but his own.

"I don't mind counting my chickens before they hatch," Chaspel went on. "I mind hatching a country chicken in the poultry deep freeze of the world. You don't understand, my profession is —"

"Jam-packed," snarled Shipoff. "Then again, as you wake me half-hourly to point out, the Holy Dinger talks to you by name; you must be one of his home yard flunkeys. Now come on Chaspel!" And he hissed in my ear, "The next time I do this, administer chloroform. Hitch? I never hitch. Rather hang by my vinyl truss plackets from a Greyhound muffler than hitch!"

On the eve of the last hundred miles, Shipoff slumped with his feet on the dashboard, flicking droppings morosely at the windshield. Every fifteen yards now, billboards, cornucopial gestalten packed with every urban succulent, whanged home to our helpless exteroceptual canisters. I sat at the window, hypnotized. Chaspel's cycles speeded up. Then he suddenly cried out, "I can't go on another mile, *igh, igh,*" cascading into gurgles. His hand clutched at his throat, missed, and socked Shipoff in the eye.

"*YOW,*" said Shipoff. "Here, here. Of course you can't." He patted the overrun tentacle between his own; in a spasm of solicitude, he actually applauded around it. "But Chaspel, you don't want to ruin the marathon anticlimax of all times with a lot of retching and roaring at the finale, do you?"

Chaspel shook his head wretchedly.

"Good boy. Let's have dinner."

"How about chicken?" I said. On the billboards perforated cheeses floated by, whorls of tuna fish, strawberry shortcakes, anything but chicken.

Chaspel pulled over. Chicken-killing time! Now this was an office which had fallen to Shipoff from the first, not only by default of Luckenkamp and me, but by his own specific zeal. But this time the future lectromagnate announced in a queer voice:

"Boys, I think I better pass."

We looked over at him, and Chaspel's face fell for the last time, reaching sea level. For all of his sufferings quailed before Shipoff's, as the iris of the lectromagnate's eyeball on the driver's side, the same Chaspel had just socked, was blown, departed, and in its place the plain eyeball gleamed white as a white star aggy.

The eye on the other side, meanwhile, was whole—in fact better than ever.

NOTA

For a thorough rundown on Shipoff's voluntary oculomotor irregularity, which became somewhat celebrated scientifically, independent of his lectromagnate career, see Annals of the B.Y. Aca. Sci., Vol. X, "Proceedings of the 7th National Institute On Strabismus and Nystagmus, Labyrinthine, Vestibular, Rotatory and Other."

Herein, enough to say that this gift was exercised by its proprietor, Shipoff, with such splendid restraint that even the exhortations of academia were as breath in a bottle: he would not do it save once a year (but not in an election year) before a discreet gathering of medical personnel, with a total interdict on photographs, motion, still, black-and-white, regardless.

Where the most compulsive show-off in Big Yolk and the city-solo picked up this lone scruple against publicity, I'll never know. May his bones be flung to the remotest khrebets of Siberia! However, where science could not prevail, how much less so the little foils and frustrations of everyday conmanship, although his career as a lectromagnate allowed no secrets, and the lectromagnate liked it that way.

Only three times, except for the benefit of science—three times in all, from beginning to end, he rolled back one eye and glorified the other.

This was the first.

That he lavished it on Chaspel will give you some idea of his mood after 3 weeks in that one's company. Two thousand miles of Luckenkamp at twenty miles an hour! After this the master refined his recoil—after this the Shipoff I came to know would have dumped the little D.D. at a bus stop in East Bulimy Court-House, with an IOU for the chickens and the deed to one glorious acre in Malaria Springs, Fla., for the car...

"I'll never forgive myself," cried Chaspel, too peeved to faint but too competitive to be left out altogether. "Isn't there something I can do?"

The white eyeball stared down kindly. "Well, what do you say *you* wring, *I* pluck?"

Whining with expectation, Chaspel dove into the trailer. Chicken-killing!—here was a nearly infallible swoon even when consciousness clave to the roof of the brain like hair-&-sealing plaster.

A few moments went by, during which Shipoff's missing iris popped playfully in and out of view. Soon Chaspel reappeared at the rear window. He 'had the carphology' but his general breakdown did not come until he had crawled halfway over the seat, so that his shoulders hung down to the seat cushions.

Then his head slipped into the crack. When the brainpan did not come free on the first attempt, it happened: he groaned, convulsed, rattled and apparently expired.

Shipoff's absconded iris rolled home for a spell, the better to take this in. "As I live and breathe," said Shipoff, "compared to this, the oft-cited doornail is a pullulating pillar of vitality."

"Get me out," Chaspel muttered. "O my chickens."

"Leave him be," Shipoff said. "This way, when tears come, he won't drown himself."

"Farsighted!" said I.

Shipoff shrugged it aside.

"Then again," I recalled, "who is to say he won't drool first?"

"Not I!" said the master. "Well bethought. Set him right."

Placed in a sitting position, Chaspel tried tearing his hair out. It hung on stubbornly. "Foul play, foul play!"

"You get used to it, my boy." Shipoff said. "A chicken has no soul."

"Two hundred chickens!"

"Brother Chaspel," Shipoff cried. "Two hundred! Two would have more than done us."

"Wiped out," moaned Chaspel. "Not a mudhen, not a booby."

"No chickens," I explained, nudging Shipoff.

"What! no chickens! Strike me blind!" His good eye went white, then both rolled home with a distant rumble. "Well either I'm very much misled, or that means no dinner."

"Gone," said Chaspel.

"Drat!" said Shipoff. "Well, small loss two hundred chickens to the poultry deep freeze of the world, but what about us, who must go without our dinner?"

On this austere note we revved up the Dodge, and proceeded in a body, nonstop now, towards Big Yolk.

III

The Depot

"I did him wrong, the time it took would shame a lesser man, but I say, On, Shipoff! courage! plough on to the next sucker. Besides in hindsight the martyroid tendencies of the little D.D. make me feel humble, a little part of nature, that is all, a mere conscript, in passing, of his persecuting Providence…"

Shipoff and I stood on a bank of the Sump, short only by its width of the first sulfurous tenements and rear lots of greater Big Yolk, watching Chaspel chug over the West Poolesville bridge to the city-solo.

"But what if he starts to sing on the sidewalk?" I said. "His blood is on our head! Let's thumb on in and save his ass."

"What? Look, starboy, it's hard enough to make a killing these hard times, without taking on a pinhead, a failure as a Fundamentalist turned chicken farmer, and already bankrupt yet. I tell you, his raw luck past and present attests a horde of afflicting stars not to be sniffed at! Think of it, all the honest hayseeds he could have picked up out there and he draws the two of us! And you want to take him in!" He struck his forehead. "When I think of the recklessness, even to ride with him all the way to the Sump! Jawbones, we're lucky to be alive."

"But you were perfection," I said.

"I thank you. Knowing how is nothing, it's keeping it up that counts. At my age I can't afford to putter around with

Luckenkamps. Don't think he won't be around for lesson two!"

Not that I really missed the Reverend Chaspel, earnest lector. It was to get there! To pull up in Big Yolk, the city-solo! To this purpose my pretexts for salvaging Chaspel had ranged from our tenth part of charity to his test-tube utility, not omitting his future as a chauffeur, as a confessor in the unlikely event of our conversion to the Chrust, as an airtight case for welfare and, of course, as a solid tax deduction. Nothing doing. "Not in my Depot!"

We stood opposed. Beyond us the Sump rolled mosquito-flecked in its trench. Behind lay a long stretch of acid pine barren, creased with superhighway, pocked with gas station. Lest they fall upon it, swarms of raindrops clung tremulously to the air. Underfoot, purslane and chicory, overhead a row of scrubby aspens—these growths and the warped remains of a trolley track divided Sump from plain.

This was the Depot—a heap of rancid earth and tin cans which, Shipoff now confessed, comprised our 'aboveground domestic commercial & professional HDQ's.' It was in its underground part, though, that the master of hindthought had made his great score. For it was no lie that Shipoff's entire fortune lay in his box in the Big Yolk P.O., the last bonus of bygone fruitful rummages through the alley of garbage cans between City Hall and Gussy's Cafeteria, in the spring of his gutter years, when the future lectromagnate lived high off the councilmen's leftover fresh ham sandwiches in the good old diet days up to Midsummer and the municipal elections. He had wiped his little mustache one day with a certain startling quitclaim...

What now lay in his P.O. box was a piece of legal parchment affirming his squatter's rights to the entire defunct subway system of outlying Big Yolk, subsequent to certain improvements. He had dutifully spread a truckload of ex-flophouse blankets on the wooden benches of the main waiting room of the West Poolesville tube. His official correspondence originated from an old fancy-carved bench in the Grand Concourse, whose moldy velvet was also his boudoir, once appointed with a gin bottle, a kerosene stove and a pyramid of Sterno cans.

The West Poolesville Depot had been a big changeover point in subway days, though subject to floods from the Sump once or twice a decade. When the BYT shut down its service, the city left the Depot to bog, eschewing title since, unless dikes were maintained, it would soon slip into the Sump.

However, the day after the land was condemned the first caravan of dumpers from West Poolesville came over the hill, the trunks of their Chevies stuffed especially with items that the city sanitation trucks left behind. The Depot was therefore preserved, not only in garbage, but in garbage man's garbage, double garbage uplifted in a can-studded pimple to the god of garbage, a miraculous levee that not only saved the Depot from the Sump, but avenged it for past inundations with a slow poisonous ooze from rotten vegetables, from the last tenant's linoleum, from old Pontiacs, dead dogs and circus turtles, from crab-infested mattresses and caved-in sofas full of rat shit.

But Shipoff's practised eye easily overshot the Depot dump and the tenements across the water, making a high centerfield fly to the heart of the matter, represented by one or two yellowish clouds on the extreme horizon. "There she lies," Shipoff said. "Now—take my bag. Good boy. Can you give haircuts? Jawbones, this flip needs trimming. Let's trade off shoes. Can you see her, starboy? That Big delicious Yolk over there! By the way, can you cook, Shamp? Don't fret, you'll learn. All in good time! Now smile, Hughby. We'll get there. In good time! There you are! A big smile for the city-solo. Two gold fillings, my boy! Why didn't you tell me? That's a sawbuck in a pinch, we'll make out, eh, starboy? Follow me!"

And he headed for the subway. I just stood there, looking at that yellow stain to the east. On that jaundiced blotch, hankering for my fillings, I was to base my leap into orthodox stoogedom till kingdom come? "Nope, I can't do it."

"I am doing it," Shipoff said, mistaking this for renewed egalitarian slobber on the Luckenkamp question. "And let me point out to you that not every upstart lectromagnate would have the balls to admit he has something to fear from hard cases.

"But starboy, this is only one instance, early in our (be it long, adoring and profitable!) acquaintance of my genuine and incontestable self-mastery."

I saw over his shoulder those iridescent coils.

"So forget about Luckenkamp. Once and for all! A harmless nobody, you call him. Yes! That he is relieved of the baggage of redeeming features we are agreed. Luckenkamp a zero—agreed! But under that zero, that featureless big top unrolling from his pole star, no girdle inhibits the concentric throbs of clunkdom he may generate, whilst he soaks up the daylight from his fellow citizens. An astrodome of nonentity fit to waterproof eastern Idaho, and you would ask him up to our Depot? I tell you a zero is a glutton! Ix-nay! Nothing doing! See my point, starboy?"

And after this off-the-cuff topical tirade he leaned in indolent recoil against an aspen, except for the eyeballs which peered at me expectantly. "Have we exhausted his possibilities as the holder of a life insurance policy, of which we would be sole beneficiaries…?"

He dismissed me with a wave. Then, whistling, he began to peel off jackets onto the bank: McCrory's Sandusky, Guido Handstitch for Porter Bros. Kansas City, Ida Seplowitz Memphis Budgeteer.

I sat, and the cold ground met my buttocks with a smack. Suddenly he turned to me again:

"Back. Back!" he repeated. "Back! Back!"

I lurched to my feet. "Back to Bulimy? Allow me to help you back to your senses. Think of my mother. To see me again would break her heart! She'd turn me in! To do the best years of my life on the county farm? No thank you. My best! But no thank you." And I trotted away down the Sumpsky Prospect, towards the West Poolesville Bridge and that yellow smudge in the distance.

A painless chop behind the knees and I was down. Looking up I saw the unmistakable contours of a hard-on behind his trouser fly, notwithstanding he had on four pairs, a tapered bulge like a radio mike, aimed on the bias at his left ear. And as I write this, the hindsight appears that maybe he was innocent, maybe it was a microphone, Shipoff being Shipoff, and never above a microphone, far from it.

All the same, I looked up at him suspiciously. His puce eyeballs were pinned sweetly and importunately to my crotch, a gaze which recalled his first gaze at me under the horse chestnut, and some of the bloom of carnal ambition it awoke in me at that time, not enough though.

"Bag! My bag!" he said gently.

I handed him his bag.

He took out a ball jar, and poured two martinis in the twilight.

So this was the track we were on. The chill of the Sumpsky Prospect soaked clean through to my homeless ass. Whoever wanted to part with his virginity when it came right down to it? Nevertheless I understood my position.

"You know which side your bread is buttered on," he whispered. "The backside! Roll over."

I considered this course reluctantly.

"Wait! Jawbones! I've got a better idea." He pulled me up, and was off again down the subway, a paved ramp like a funnel. "Follow me."

A thin stripe of twilight supported my nervous steps like a banister. All at once it died away.

Now I have always feared the dark. No doubt I always will. And for good reason, here amply borne out, believe me.

Suddenly the future lectromagnate's voice closed in from all sides at once, very loud, yet faraway:

am

where

I   ?

My throat closed with a click. I snatched at the rhythmic

26

dust parading up my retinae, yelled, gagged, and bailed out on the floor.

Lights came on. I sat up in an enormous empty vault of yellow tile, marred only by Shipoff at the far end, his hand on a switch box, stark naked. "Alive after all?" he sneered. "Too bad. I thought you might have an excuse." And he flicked his crumpled cock. "Granted my taste is my own. I do like my fun."

I made a few apologetic remarks, which he ignored. "Got no time for you! I'll go cop a sure thing, a few shots and a nickel sheeny pickle." He knotted his tie, a rosy taffeta number. "I'm off to Big Yolk. Hold the roundhouse."

"Take me!"

"Take you!" he snapped. "What have you ever done for me?"

"Anything!"

He sniggered. "Your watch, for example?

My regretted father's railroad Longines! Now, I was not below a little sentiment in my youth. I had had a little diamond stud, for instance, which my mother had given me after my first date. The contortions of mendacity I had had to sustain in order to keep it without ever going on another had made it a holy relic.

(Nevertheless it disappeared the night when, insensible to threats, I spent the four full hours of the Daughters of the Eastern Star "Miss Bulimy" pageant in the bathtub, steaming off Brakeknot's latest score.)

I confess that my papa's old railroad Longines, on the other hand, was of value strictly material, a hundred dollars, and still rising, at its latest assessment.

I cleared my throat.

Shipoff, dressed to kill, paced up and down worse than any lion—a bellboy weaned on the Big Yolk baksheesh circuit.

I sneezed.

"Besonnenheit!"

"Thanks but no thanks," said I.

"What is a watch to a young man whose fiscal future is precision clockwork?"

"Details?"

"Longines?"

We glared at one another. "No, stop right there," he said at length, patting my buttocks, smoothing my lapel: "Your peevishly reactionary kink in our imperturbably progressive corpus is like Mrs. Lurleen Stump nee Grossnickel stinting on sirloin for cheerios when the boxtop offer has already expired. What Lurleen has not, how can anyone take away from her?

"She ought to get back in circulation! If I'm not back by midnight, try living without me." With that he threw the switch and went, his footsteps dying on the dark before his ragged laughter.

"Resolved,"—(said Shipoff)—"the timeliest *topos*, via the slickest *tropos*, from the loftiest lecterns; the best-looking lectors, all cut to my butt, and plenty of toadies for matters of no importance. A hot line to the Arslevering clan paymaster..." He was drunk; he had been drinking for five days and six nights, not excluding the sabbath. O the sabbath came on, stared, and wandered away. Monday was dawning. There had been an unseasonable freeze in the night, and in the early hours I prowled around West Poolesville for a Sunday edition.

Chaspel Luckenkamp's undersized head suddenly appeared around the upramp as I lay on the floor in dejection, wrapped in the Sports section. Shipoff on his bench groaned out of Real Estate, stuck by the first thin beams from the skylight. "Now then!" said Chaspel. "I was wondering..."

Shipoff belched, floundered onto his back, with a face like an untied horsefeed sack. He recognized Chaspel. "Honorary doctor Luckenkamp! So soon! How was Big Yolk?"

"Promising." Chaspel drew a little memo pad in rainbow colors out of his carpet bag. "I would like to have your reflections on, aaa, where to start. When to stop. Also when to start and where to stop. Who to call. Why to call whom, also what to say, when. Also… "

Shipoff faked a snore.

"As I suspected, the buzzard sleeps late."

"Lest he scarf up a tapeworm like you, brother Chaspel."

Chaspel turned and yanked me up out of the Sports section. For a bantamweight evangelist, he could muster a wild-eyed recoil. "Make him help me. I'm down to my last ten. What do I do?"

"Could you lend me a fin?" I suggested, as his ear was so convenient. He stepped away from me aghast, and none too soon, as Shipoff's empty Pinsk bottle sailed through the interval.

"Honorary Luckenkamp, if I lie here drunk as a landlord, don't be misled, it was only by the charity of my handmaiden Hughbury, charity not only unwilling but damn near unable, I mean unforgivable charity in terms of its low cash value at the hock shop."

"Tragic!" I said.

"Yes! and fast exhausted. You see I pinched his pocket watch, I translated the meager swag into a bare week's necessities, to wit, a half case of rotgut vodka, a blow job at the art flic, a few weenies with kraut, and a shoeshine." He held up his well-travelled cordovans. "Oh yes, and the punk threw the clap in free, I just pay for the penicillin. Also that was my last bottle. Now, was this bliss, Chaspel, or was it the pastewax veneer of bliss in its fleetingest scintillation? And you cry help you. Better help me!"

Chaspel began knotting a noose out of his greasy necktie.

"O no, Luckenkamp, no need to rush into things. You're still ten berries to the good. Wait till you beat around the city-solo flat broke for a few weeks, then at least it would be reasonable, even profound! Okay, okay. No doubt we should help Reverend Luckenkamp, Hughby, as he once helped us. You know where the bag is, bring me the Manual."

29

Off I went. Ravens wheeled in the spare equinoctial sunlight over the Sumpsky Prospect, spotting carrion. A starling skreed in the aspens, then I heard—unearthly singing.

✧ ✧ ✧

"Yoo hoo," cried Shipoff. It was full day. Sunbeams flitted in brilliant rods over the concourse walls, by, I now saw, the agency of a glass thermometer protruding from Shipoff's buttocks. Chaspel was gone. "Didn't I say he'd be back? What a zero! Actually the energy of that down-and-out chawbacon inspires me to action. O I'm not sick," he said as I stared. "Would I were! God knows I tried."

"Where's Chaspel?"

"I told him to get into the Arslevering open house this week with his collar, work his way to the front and then sing at the top of his lungs."

"What will they do with him?"

"Hang him, maybe. Get me page 21."

They were all blank. Shipoff held a match under page 21. A phone number appeared in a tall unsteady hand.

"Dr. Harry Analarge. A dear dear friend of Mrs. Arslevering, and a complete bug. Now I myself never met the man. I have, yes, had some relations with his family, who all do it like pigs. Meaning one long dribble from dusk till dawn, during which they grunt bits of useful information in your ear, like their famous Uncle Analarge's telephone number in Big Yolk. The object"—he yawned—"to prolong your disinterest without arousing your actual hostility… by Chrust it works. Later they tell you he's a few bricks short of a load, in fact, soft as a grape for years!" He shrugged, pulling a dime out of his pocket. "O well, a man who can write prescriptions is nothing to sneeze at, provided his ballpoint's in the right place, the schmeer pot, for instance. And Mrs. Arslevering's cultural advisor, after all? Besides I like plastic surgeons, they're optimists at heart, they take measures!"

He thinks of everything, I thought.

30

"Here then is a useful telephone number. It's a B.Y. exchange, it didn't come cheap. Question is, will I rise to the occasion.

"Why rise when I can extend to the occasion? You, little Hughby, will run to the West Poolesville PURE OIL, find a phone booth, dial this number, ask for..."

IV
Dr. Analarge

I was a success. From our first telephone conversation, Dr. Analarge told me everything. It was only later I learned that Dr. Analarge told everybody everything, and, what was more, told everything differently every time he told it.

But I had the honor to report to Shipoff, after our fifth lengthy phonecall: "The doctor says that the tape recorders in the steam ducts have been taken away, but they're buzzing his laboratory now with helicopters all day long, from nine to 5:30, with an hour off for lunch—he eats at the same hour, whatever it is. That does it, he says—he's moving here Tuesday."

Shipoff rose to his feet. To him this great triumph was occasion for anything, even sobriety. I therefore mixed the "Eight Ounce Cure," the privilege of whose preparation fell to me throughout our acquaintance.

When we were friends no more, I knew from the Cure better than to squander poison on Shipoff.

To a ball jar:

One part kerosene	*Dash liquid wrench*
Two parts boiling water	*1 tbsp. Malagasi chutney*
	Dollop corn plaster
Juice of a lemon	*Pulp of one beef heart*
¼ tsp. Aleppo red pepper	*Sterno to taste*

Shipoff drank, shook my hand, and fell unconscious for 36 hours, rising clear-headed at dawn Tuesday with a violent lurch and the words, "I kiss your foot." So far so good. He puttered around the subway vaults till noon, when he emerged with the Aries imprint deepening in his brow and equipage for two as follows: lemon kid gloves, silk bow-ties, wing-tips, black-tipped canes; a vintage Alto Douro, Penang patchouli in bulbous atomizers, studs of jaundiced crystal, camellia button-holes and two pounds of chocolate-covered orange peel in a gilt basket.

A moving van rolled up the Sumpsky Prospect that after-noon about 3:00; by dawn it was gone and the prefabricated house and laboratory stood shining in its place. A white build-ing, overnight on the Depot dump! I saw the first signs of trouble on Shipoff's face. Meanwhile the doctor's feet and other goods and chattels declined to appear, to be kissed or for any other purpose. Shipoff sent over his card and the week's best crossword puzzles, in vain. No word.

Then suddenly, Friday morning, invitations to a dinner-concert in the doctor's quarters appeared on the subway upramp, weighted, for it was windy, with strings of rock candy.

At this novel yet nostalgic touch, Shipoff almost faltered. Then he righted himself: "Starboy, Shipoff has lost the setting, not the scene. Who can rise can extend to the occasion. Mean-while, a certain adaptability is god-uncle to the art. He's moved in at least—he can stake us to dinner, it's cheaper this way."

The most ensnarled and aggravated of egotists, Shipoff had as a rule the mastery of his mania; when it served him, he could affect an almost maidenly forbearance. He had taken pains to inform himself of the doctor's international connections, his imprudent investments, Scandinavian bank accounts, his in-fluence on the Arslevering heiress whose figurative tit nursed the Big Yolk artistic community, his compulsive eating, his solitudinous domestic habits, and his chronic dementia paranoides, with fugue.

He knew also of the doctor's pea vines, violets, potted marjoram, his yarns and knitting needles, and his private loft above the laboratory block, reached by two holes in the ceiling, a rope ladder (up), a pole (down), the ladder detachable, the pole greased, of his short-lived secretaries, of his adored daughter Annie.

Thus primed, Shipoff intended to set out his coils with a delicate hand, to embrace the doctor's happiness.

In the end the doctor's failure to appear goaded Shipoff to war. Friday evening we knocked at the laboratory vestibule. The doctor's long-legged buck-toothed secretary, Reddick, took our coats. Behind him forty dinner guests milled around in the cigar smoke. As for the doctor, Reddick said he was "resting," but "might turn up, with luck."

"That does it!" Shipoff's fingers pressed his eyes in two little baskets. We moved to our seats. "This is war, Hughby. A misfortune, a waste, but what can I do?"

"He does have something bugging his head, don't you think? The helicopters buzzing his limousine? Video-tapes in the wallpaper?"

Shipoff never heard me. "And he's watching me, the Chrust! I can feel his eyeballs boring into my back like a pair of handlebars." Sweeping aside his place setting, Shipoff recklessly thrust a whole Madras hot pepper into his jaws and presently fell to the floor, thrashing like a snake in rut until with index finger and a hherk that echoed down the laboratory block he got it down.

Most of the company looked at him briefly, but as for him, he only looked at me. Tipping forward in my chair, I read his gaze:

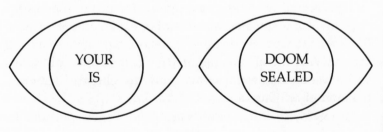

YOUR
IS

DOOM
SEALED

"Now wait a minute, Sergei. Why me?"

"Why? You're all I've got." He stood, brushed his lapels with his handkerchief, nodded all around. "Well, I'm through with this shindig. It's all yours now. You got him on the phone. Piss on him!" He paused a moment, then repeated: "You can piss on him. In fact, do piss on him, on him and his party or don't come home at all, hear?"

This was Brakeknot's fame, not mine, even in absentia. "You think that's all I can do," I said. "I might as well go back to Bulimy as get stuck on that track for life."

Shipoff struck himself in the forehead. "I wanted a real flunkey when I picked you up, not a union shop. Now come on Hughby! I don't have all night."

"Try bribery," I said. "That always works."

"What'll you have?"

"How about the three-dollar tour of metropolitan Big Yolk?"

The lectromagnate fished in his jacket and flashed below the tablecloth a map of the BYT subway network, which he had no doubt been packing for just such a contingency.

I snatched it up. The city-solo! Shipoff smiled, nodded all around and bowed out backwards. The door to the vestibule woofed shut behind him.

First I looked over the map. Of course all the tubes led to Big Yolk, where else? What a clunk I was not to have trotted on down one, one day. But the far tunnels were as blind as mole holes, and in the dark I could hear the river hissing over my head…

Then I looked over the guests. For the purpose I had the long spell of the doctor's international dinner. Someone pointed to the doctor's daughter Annie—certainly she stood out among the guests without any assistance, under a hive of yellow corkscrew curls that guaranteed a freewheeling disposition. As a matter of fact, her dinner neighbor Leftwich Proctor (later a lector) had his face half-hidden in the purplish fichu where her bosoms were roosting, and was bobbing up and down with her kazoo between his teeth, then going down to come up with some other doodad—a tortoise shell pick, rubber band, a crumpled dollar bill.

Outside of that interesting couple, the dinner guests laid no stress on the bounds of decorum. Like me, they spent most of the supper hour staring at Annie. I compared their more obvious talents to mine. This occupation, good as a rule for a couple hours of obsession plus the same again in matching depression, tonight soon creaked to a halt. They had no talents I could get hold of, for money blipped off their several pelts with deafening uniformity.

At last the concert began.

> *Well I got one in Alabama*
> *I got one in Loosiana*
> *Got one in Texarkana*
> *One in Corsicana*

Fraulein Analarge drank straight corn liquor without letting down her electric guitar. She was a formidable soloist, though her playing was only so-so.

> *One in Indiana*
> *Nineteen in Tennessee*
> *I wants another half a dozen*
> *Just to run around with me*

Just then Doctor Analarge slipped in. He moved, fat as he was, so swiftly that my chance to piss on him was blown before the door shut behind him. His face was colored with a mixture of paternal jealousy and territorial pride, as he crossed toward a hassock at the foot of the bandstand. My right hand went to my fly, while with the left I raised my glass to the back of my neighbor's neck and drank: "To the city-solo!" She turned round, looked me over, then winked on a tortuous bias—this was Yeeza Ames, future Depot duplicating department chairwoman, president of AUNTY, guardian of the mad.

I hastened to the door. Chrust! Through the hole I had for a pocket, the transit system map caught in my fly. A minute passed in the tussle. By then Annie was riffing with three amplifiers. Half the audience were holding their ears. Of course the piss sparkled inaudibly down to the linoleum. I watched the sleek backs of forty-one heads. Dr. Analarge had waded long since to his little hassock, and sat staring at Annie through the restless streams of spotlights, apparently oblivious. Only Annie, still riffing, eyed me dispassionately from the band-stand. Then—the door was bolted! I panicked and rattled the knob, which brought Reddick toeing like a crane through the cigar smoke.

"What? Leave?" he whispered, seizing my elbow. "Please, please, the fraulein is so sensitive!" He stuck one of the doctor's famous Jamaican perfectos in my mouth, lit it, and pushed me into my seat.

Still winking, Yeeza Ames took up her goblet: "Same to you, honey," she said. "And thanks."

The waa-waa of the amplifiers ebbed to the pitch of wind ringing in the aspens on the Sumpsky Prospect. The insomniac rustle of autumn was afoot, endowing me as usual with a vague, nostalgic sense of doom in the body. Adjusting the controls between her feet, Fraulein Analarge pulled her frock over her knees, then in sudden impatience pushed the whole skirt through the back of her chair. She wore no panties. The dinner guests stared at that red snapper cunt, flashing like a garnet in a hedge of kelp. "Bravo," sighed young Leftwich. His forelock was floating in his liqueur. The doctor sobbed out loud—but then, I had been hearing his melodious tears for the last two selections.

Annie plucked into tune a diminished sonority, small, flat and bell-like. The skirt rolled down. She sang. It was a little ditty, the accompaniment a spare, follow-the-dots horizon of unstrained counterpoint:

> *All is caduke*
> *All disappears*

Dr. Analarge gasped distinctly.

While the peacock displays
My papa disports
Defective from birth
From his knees to his ears

Dr. Analarge pulled the amplifier plug out of the wall in a sudden lunge. "What more can I say," he cried, "than welcome and please yourselves?" He hastened to stick between his teeth a Jamaican Melody No. 1; nevertheless, his eyes were full of tears. An old lady crept towards him with her hanky. "Rubbish, Charlotte," he said, pushing it away, "I'm used to it, used to it."

His complexion was Mediterranean, save for the skin of his scalp, lines of which shown so whitely through dark hair that it seemed stitched on in segments. His features were small and fine, but lay like a clutch of pullet eggs in a nest of fat from brow to jowls and lapping over his collar. Yet he was somehow handsome, and had a birthmark in the old sense, such as sets one apart for grand rotations on the turbine of fortune: a large, star-shaped mole on his Adam's apple.

In addition the interior of his mouth was apple-green, though whether from something he had eaten that night, from disease, or the lighting, I cannot say.

V

Annie

Doctor Analarge approached me soon enough, working himself down the banquet table with one hand along the edge. Thank god I hadn't pissed on him. A childless uncle's face, indulgent and sorrowful. Taking Reddick's arm he drew him along. "My prop in time of illness"—he meant me—"meet my millstone." The millstone held out two freckled fingers.

"Your prop!" I said. "You exaggerate."

"Not at all."

"And how are you now, Dr. Analarge?"

"It didn't kill me." The doctor wiped his eyes on a table napkin and moved to the window, tacking slightly.

"Is this amazing, Reddick! a subway dump yet!"

"I've seen it, doctor," the secretary said sourly.

The doctor pointed his thumb at him umpire-style. "A verschlepteh krank! Who needs him. But my daughter says, sign up that Texas beanpole, papa, I could wrap my legs around him twice. What could I say? I'm an indulgent father. But what a state I've been in ever since. Nor can a state be empty but these reel on and on, Hughby…" He scratched his head. "Here's how it goes. One day a taxi I'm in drives up some country lane I've never clapped eyes on before, so I think. Or maybe it's the lobby of some two-horse town deadfall; I'm coming through the doorway—*fech!* I come to composition. Awake for a change!

Just like that! For why I don't know. And what do I see? O, Reddick playing solitaire on the vanity table, smoking my cigars and whistling *Kansas City Kitty!* Reddick in the front seat shelling peanuts for the cabby! saying, 'Drive, pal, just drive and charge it to the doctor.' Reddick on his twin bed in the Cozy Grove Motel, watching Rhonda Fleming and pulling it, four horsepower."

"Lord!" cried Reddick out the north window.

"Yes!" said the doctor. "And who wouldn't go buggy around you everyday. But I hang on a little while, you know why? To see my little Annie. Where is my daughter? Come here, precious girl." He ran his hand over her hair, that small cluster he could reach, of bright gold curls like springs. "Yellow hair, what do you think of her, Hughby? A gifted girl, an enterprising girl." He patted her rearend; she groaned and walked away. "I've let her do mostly what she wants in life," he went on, "a mistake! But you can't restore the unspoiled state just like that! And if you could, can a state be empty? She had a mind of her own from birth. And permit me to say in my behalf that if you permit everything, you get at least an honest answer. Watch this...darling Anneleh!"

Coming back she curled a long arm around the doctor's neck; it hung over his shoulder, ending in five red nails. "Yanneleh, why don't you give up that filthy hair oil business and work for me in the lab? You know you wouldn't want for a thing."

She ran her hand over his head. "*Lieber* papa, you know I can't take you for more than 45 minutes at a time. Besides— what was that?" She paused, listening. A distant tinkle: two tiny lights leaped in her eyes, like fleas.

"*Hist!* where have I seen that face," cried the doctor—"her dead mother, listening for coins in the upper story! She's her mother's child, a pointed tendency, *regardez*, to look for gelt at the most meagre exteroceptive stimulus. No time for me! but did you see those eyes? she was hearing dimes and quarters. Admit it, Yanneleh! Your mother—"

"Was she really a wetnurse?"

"Did I ever say so? No, that was a lie. She was a born cashier. The embezzling instinct set in at the median age—35. Until then she wouldn't have helped herself to a chopstick, so pure was her identification with the management. A flunkey without fault, she loved her work. In that strain, my dear, the lethal quirk will always out before quitting age, one of those truth-bearing potboilers I'm always talking about, a late bloomer, but a hanging offense in Kentucky.

"Your mother was a beautiful woman," the doctor went on, "like you, very like! But the elastic hairnet she was forced to wear on the job all those years gave her face, in the end, a peculiar twist hindmost, like that of one sent through the air at sixty or seventy miles an hour once a day, against keen and vigorous protestations...

"Perhaps that slight disfigurement helped turn her around in the end. Yet whatever its toll on her nosebulb and temples, the manager of the hash house who found her out was still crazy in love with her. He interested her not at all! He begged! He would cover for her, she need only move in with him, he'd pay for everything, he had a furnished ten-by-ten over a Chinese hand laundry. She refused. He cried. Then let her just give back the money and clear out of the state. She said it was spent.

"She asked to be strung up in her cashier's uniform. The black peau de soie hung a little lower on the left hand side than the right, my child"—the doctor flattened Annie's tit with his large miller's thumb—"like so. What heart! It seems she had devised a little swag bag for that place. It was stuffed with cash! She had had a breast removed for the purpose."

"O ridiculous, she must have had cancer," Reddick said.

"For the purpose!" shouted the doctor. "I am in a position to know. She was a single-minded cashier, strong-headed. I loved her. She never spent a dime, it was all there. A martyr, a real rebel, the heroic function in the feminine mode: all concealed gains and unconcealable decompensations.

"So you see, little Annie, you have it easy. Come live with me."

41

"An hour of you, pop, is the limit!" said she.

"You can see why I have to indulge her," said the doctor. "I'm afraid she would leave me completely. She would leave me I know!"

Reddick, who had stood the while at the north window, suddenly put his fist through the pane. That entire section of the prefabricated laboratory wall then tottered and went down, and the secretary walked calmly out into the night and down the Sumpsky Prospect. The squad of Depot toadies picking over the banquet table looked up in shock, naturally enough, and for that moment the melodious chink of crystal on flatware went still. "Continue!" said the doctor, rapping the table with his fist. He grabbed Annie at the waist: "Shall we? I think it's a cha-cha." The toadies cleared on, only louder.

I'd had enough. "Perhaps three is a crowd?" I said, backing towards the exit.

"One is a crowd!" said the doctor, dancing. "Three is beyond all relation."

"Good night, doctor."

"O but Shamp!" I was halfway through the hole that Reddick had made when he called out. "Shamp, one thing! Why O why did you piss on my new linoleum? A discouraging sight! No, let it go by. That's what I was saying, little Anneleh. Confusion unmans, yes! But it's waking that kills you. You never catch up. Now why did he do that to me? Well, go home. My best to Shipoff... No wait." He suddenly galloped down the laboratory block towards me with his arms outstretched, moving his grand bulk so easily and quietly that I thought of a tree, deep in snowy foliage.

Then he stopped in front of me, but again turned and spoke to Annie. "No, I can't help it. Now how do you explain that, my tsotske, all over my new... Wait," for I'd started away again. "Why all that piss? Something to do with those ears?"

Ears?

"*Fech*, I thought so!" he said, and he tweaked one.

My hands flew to my ears. A soft and nerveless appendage

wobbled from each lobe. I ran to the vestibule mirror, and there they were, bobbing a little, red as cockscombs.

"An ear-wattled pisser, I swear to my god," said the doctor. Then with a sigh, he heaved himself up the ropes.

VI
The Star Topos

Besides the shock of the ear wattles, I now had to contend with the rage of the master who had left me to piss on Dr. Analarge on pain of banishment.

But next morning I had a piece of luck—before it was mine it was Shipoff's. At dawn the future lectromagnate was pacing the passageway between the upramp and the Grand Concourse, waiting to collar me for my showing in last night's hostilities. "Chrust! Where is that mortal flubber?" I was crouching in an old telephone booth a little ways down the chute, watching the dawn harp coldly over the iron grating behind his head. Meanwhile the look I read on his face was the best of arguments yet for a running dash for the city-solo, now that my subway map was in my pocket, without lengthy farewells, had it not been for one nagging presentiment: I should stick with the master. For—a fag of cold-blooded habits, Shipoff, but, please observe, a man of parts.

For example, his choice of a topos.

The topos that Shipoff had the eyeballs to pursue, sew up and make his middle name, and from which he would soon ship out the first crop of fledgling lectors to lecterns in Big Yolk, Little Athens, Hinnstead and points west, was the Population Detonation.

There was nothing to argue in the fact of the burgeoning

crowd itself, of course. But Shipoff was the first, and the last, to rifle obsolete periodical files, dissolved committee transcripts and tabloid morgues for novel, obscure and unpopular proposals for stemming it. Whence this passion for theoretical rejects? They were dirt cheap. He was a man who had not had an idea of his own in his life. Fine with him! Instead he rutted and ransacked in the surplus heap under cover of the public yawn, as sure that the plan he wanted would out as though he smelled it, rotting already from delay, behind its binder in the library basement. By his nose he would find the idea that, properly dressed and delivered, could be forked into the public yawn by the bushelful, to the glory of the Depot, the art and his own lectromagnate career.

Sure enough, in a compendium of *Exempla For Now* by the much-quoted but shadowy World-Friar Tapsvine, Shipoff turned up a model, "Courtship and Estivation Among Aswan Crocodiles," describing the rip-roaring mating habit of that saurian subsequent to (but intimately connected with) his protracted retreat to the slime. Tapsvine constructed an analogy in which human populations upgraded the quality of their vice along similar lines, first trading unlimited freedom for a season of "total involvement," then retrieving purity and youth, after it was done, by abstinence, solitude, and a long rest in mud.

This plan had many selling points to be sure, notably its aphrodisiac insinuation. But Tapsvine had enemies in the bastions of leftover morality, diehards from conventional congregations of Chrust, on the right hand, and ethical greenards from Re-Natured Reasoning study groups on the left. Radical elements of both these parties were strongly represented on opening day at the Arslevering Annual "Little Athens" Ox Roast and Colloquium on Polity. Here the World-Friar first aired his idea.

Trouble followed.

Under intense questioning, Tapsvine admitted that, what though everybody should, still everybody could not hibernate as yet, owing to insufficient facilities. Then who exactly was to be buried, asked the greenards, and with what guarantees? What better way to "bury" your political adversaries than to bury them indeed: invoking their civic duty to hibernate, to defer their causes till spring, then throw away the shovels? And were citizens A and B seriously to abstain in their holes from October to April, while citizens C, D and Tapsvine frisked around the upper world banging like bunnies?

A bomb went off the second morning of the Colloquium in the outdoor toilets, showering the hornbeam grove with turds and wet paper. The World-Friar had just banged the door behind him, having had breakfast five minutes earlier than usual owing to the perfect weather. He walked straight to the speakers' banquet table without visible fear.

"Do it all year, kiddies—be my guests," he said, and he vanished. Reports followed that he had resumed the pluralist moralist's wanderings on which his legend was largely based, with the temporary additions of a bulletproof underfrock and a strapping ex-Vegas bouncer named Henny. He had been last seen among the Tupí remnant, in the Amazon headwaters west of Manaus.

The near-fatal Ox Roast was five years gone. Somehow, despite his clerical garb and long disappearances, he maintained the reputation of a man of fashion.

Looking backwards upon Tapsvine's proposal, Shipoff was intrigued, in the crocodile passage, by "protracted retreat," the coil and recoil of massive populations. It was easy to see that if half the people could be induced to snore while the other half went about their business, the population bomb would be defused overnight, at least for a couple of lifetimes. Best of all, this respite could be arranged without forcing any real change in the aboveground, day-to-day habits of huge and recalcitrant populations.

Shipoff discovered a selling point too in the suggestion, "retrieving purity and youth." Aside from cosmetic benefits, there was a secret message for every marital partner: if an uninteresting spouse could be persuaded to drop down the

shaft at the first ho-hum, the divorce rate would yield at last—
to separate hibernation cycles. There was even a slice of bait for
the submerged prudery of the Re-Natured Reasoners who had
made Big Yolk too hot for Tapsvine five years before, in the
hint of a revival of strictly seasonal breeding.

Lastly, if we had nothing else at the Depot, we had plenty of
holes to hibernate in.

So a future was assured to the lector who would argue the
case before the world for voluntary ("holiday") hibernation
with sexually recharging properties, or alternatively for chemi-
cally-induced dormancy—the kind that Tapsvine had had in
mind—astrodisiac hibernation, months of nod drenched with
inexpressibly beautiful hallucinatory entertainment. And this
was the spiel that revolved in my mind as I squatted in the
phone booth to Shipoff's rear. Meanwhile the master was so
impatient for my appearance that from time to time he popped
a fist, *clup!* on my absent ear.

Whatever my future, the present encouragements left me
cold.

More than once I took my mark on Big Yolk. Down the tubes
then! But just as it fixed on the pinprick of light at the end of the
subway tunnel, my mind's eye would roll sideways to a hall of
well-washed ears straining toward my lit-up lectern, their programs squashed to knots, their fingers aching to sign themselves down the hole with the first—

Suddenly Reddick's freckled face appeared at the upramp,
blue with exertion and distress. "The doctor's going corko
again. I quit! He's billed to talk at the Arsleverings' tonight, but
he can get there without me. I'm not pushing 300 pounds of
badmouth down those tubes dolly or no dolly. If he won't go
quietly he won't go at all." Reddick sat down on the concrete
and buried his face in his hands. "The things he says!"

"We can't blow the Arsleverings," Shipoff said. "The doctor
must go."

"I quit! You take him."

"Tut! just like that! What's the topos?"

"The population de—"

"Jawbones!" Shipoff stuck out a gloved hand. "Done! Just button the doctor in his best duds before you take off. We'll get him there all right." Reddick bounded away.

And now Shipoff praised his luck. He praised it to the domes, the rails and floor tiles of the whole defunct BYT, to the Depot skylights, and to the river groaning in its bed:

"Laud, laud, fortune is form. Whatever comes off, works. Omit no luck! For when I lay me down in the gutter for want of a four-bit bed in which to spend the night, I laud! For who knows what embarrassing blurb may be posted that evening just under my mugshot in the lobby of my favorite flophouse, Hinky's La Ritz? All weather and all luck I laud, I laud my life, in the infinite enjoyability of revolving…" And my crime forgotten, his pink satin waist cinch newly snapped to his gills, Shipoff spun up the ramp into daylight.

By St. Cornwallis! Impressive and sound as these sentiments were, I must point out that, throughout my acquaintance with the lectromagnate—may his bones starve the weevils of a dwindling generation—he was never moved to laud his bad luck until, as today, he had ample good luck to chase it with.

Hibernator's Antiphon

Why hibernate?	*Why not?*
EEYOW	*io hiberna*
Shall men change?	*Haw-haw!*
Though thou'lt burst?	*Hip-hip*
[ALL] **THEY STAY THE SAME**	
The natural coil...	*Recoil*
in our extremity	*Recess*
in our simplicity	*same...*
[ALL] **THEY STAY THE SAME**	
Same!	*Hip-hip*
HIBERNA	*for room*
VAROOM	*harem*
HAROOMBOOM	*hiberna*
GIVE ROOM	*¡Hola!*
Hollow!	*cave room*
KAVROOM	*bar room*
BARROOM	*cave room bar room*
O Hole!	*Kaboom!*

In a solidly rising wall of weal... *IO HIBERNA!*
The unstoppable well well-stopped *IO HIBERNA!*

[ALL] **GIVE ROOM**
FOR ROOM
VAROOM
KAVROOM
HAROOM
BARROOM

An A-o!	*An EEyow!*
An I-o!	*A You-o!*
[ALL] **A Why-o!**	
Io hiberna?	*Hibernacula io!*
[ALL] **HIBERNACULA!**	

49

VII

The Arslevering Wing-Ding

On top of all their other falling points, the Arsleverings could be lavish. So Reddick advised me, as he lugged his suitcase away down the Sumpsky Prospect. The Arslevering compound was laid out on reclaimed tar bubbles of the Great Morass at the city center, Big Yolk. Over this priceless tuft, the white stuccoed quartermile of balustraded pueblo which the Arsleverings called home, or "Little Athens," was crocheted to its kiosked gardens by a spidery radial floodlight affair, unrolling on these bi-weekly "occasions" with all the wall-eyed jazz of a Big Yolk used car lot.

The Arsleverings also took plummets, according to my advance information, for (a) their unsusceptibility to merit without celebrity, and (b) their equally unremitting horror of missing anything. As a result of this combination, at every flap of fashion in Big Yolk, the standing roster of Arslevering dependents quaked in a body, an aspen in the same fickle gust that inspired the patrons to new fits of prodigality.

Control of the Arslevering piecrust fortune was presently vested in the 35-year-old heiress who was throwing this party. A former international daredevil, Vasselina was said to have paid her way into the original Baghdad games, but her showing in later meets was not unrespectable. At least she made up in ballistic capability what she lacked in wits, or perhaps she had willfully sacrificed such brains as she possessed at the outset to the cause of logging in ever more violent and bizarre concussions.

In any event it was Doctor Analarge who had been called upon so many times to restore her face and physique, if not to normal, at least to easy recognition by others of the species. She had begun taking dares so early in life that it was vain to speculate upon what she had looked like from nature. And the doctor had long since given up trying to preserve a semblance, in each new face, of any of her previous reconstructions. But their long working partnership had given Doctor Analarge, when lucid the kindest of men, a free entry into the Arslevering household. Once there, kindest or meanest, so long as a person had brains enough to pick through the TV listings in the Big Yolk paper, he was drafted into an advisorial position.

We hung around the gate. All at once the doctor, looking east, gesticulated excitedly. We looked over. On the crest of a geyser of skyblue streamers our hostess was approaching, Vasselina Arslevering in butting posture, full throttle. Her course was set on Shipoff.

I jerked him behind the stone riser of a footbridge. For all at once I remembered Reddick's warning, as he jumped up and down on his suitcase and scattered his six months' pay stubs from the doctor into the Sump, that, acute in little else, Vasselina had an unfailing eye for a bugger, overt, closet, reformed, retired, regardless, at fifty paces, and this eye was inhospitable. But the doctor's secretary had also called over his shoulder the classical tactic for the engagement: "Don't come up swinging: pinch her fanny." I passed on Reddick's advice to my colleagues.

"Ah yes, Reddick," said the doctor, wiping his glasses as Vasselina gained on the inner gate in a cloud of dust. "A verschlepteh krank! but he was, in his day, the most collected of navigators."

Our hostess veered off the limestone, righted herself and plucked Shipoff up by the lapels. "Who's daring me to drop this seedy faggot down the cistern? Do I hear twenty-five cents?" With her left foot she actually raised a rustic manhole cover. ("Is it a well?" "Jawbones, a very well indeed.") "Any pal of yours is a pal of mine, doc," she went on, "but by Jesus I've had it up to here with visionary cornholers cruising my old man, soaking up my booze, oowoo…" We all tweaked her butt at once, seeing Shipoff dangle so insecurely over the well from her forefingers. She went rigid and fell like a tree trunk.

"Twenty-five cents!" Shipoff nudged her toward the open hatch with his cordovans. "As you would be cherished, so cherish, madame."

"Any pal? visionary?" The doctor now corrected his patient dutifully, though late. "No, Vasselina, this is the gay impresario Shipoff, lectromagnate, personality, publicist, snake, who sets out his coils to round up your foggy and crepitous visionary types, who keep abreast of their times, though arrears in all else…"

A champagne tray went by and Shipoff followed it into the crowd. As he picked off a glass someone cried, "Yevlenkovich!"

At the name I perceived a tremor pass over the lectromagnate. Hindthought assures me he felt no fear but came up coldblooded, flexing his well-packed coils. A young man with Arkansas blue eyes, a scribble of golden hair on his chest and lobed, perfect thighs under a St. Tropez G-string, plunged out of the crowd in his direction. If Shipoff was steady, the newcomer shook like an old Bowery winesoak at the reins of a temperance bandwagon. But his hand was firm around Shipoff's elbow.

Shipoff turned with a puzzled expression.

"Ten years to the day, Vassily Yevlenkovich, I hunted you. And now you walk through the gate like…the same old Yevlenkovich, artist, importer, *periodista*, officer, drama coach, *comme vous voulez*, doing a little business with this one and that one, not even here to see McCorkle."

Shipoff peered at him, then smiled. "Well, you've got a muzhik sure enough, comrade, but not the party wanted I'm afraid. Sergei Shipoff"—he stuck out his hand—"topical tirader? centrifugal tropist? Doctor Analarge's colleague and, ah, lesser known cousin?"

"Don't be foolish, Yevlenkovich. I forgave you long since." McCorkle's transparent eyes picked out Vasselina coming to on the turf and he pointed at her. "See that? She listens to me. Vassily Yevlenkovich, say you know me. I'll do what I can for you, just put my mind at ease. What do you say to two hundred and fifty million dollars, *querido?*" He led Shipoff off by the elbow. "I said yes. Not the classical system for keeping the vessel within a man unclogged for the conduct of philosophy..." They strolled arm in arm along the bog bank; I followed along dog-like. "It seemed like a good idea at the time. But the woman hangs on so tight!"

Shipoff shrugged. "You know how the rich stay rich."

"What? O the money! Never mind the money, anything I say—dog museums, pharmaceutical factories, mail order porn flics, anything. A small New England town for a John Baptist day bonfire...check! Two million point five for the Theater of the People of Barney Street Big Yolk, I got it. But fifteen minutes alone in the craphouse with the Y.C.O.R. manual and a bottle of beer, that's another ballgame." They strode in silence along the footbridges. Still Shipoff listened indulgently. "With you, I could handle her. Can you see it, Yevlenkovich?"

Shipoff smiled vaguely. To be Yevlenkovich or not to be Yevlenkovich: once two hundred and fifty million clams had entered the arena, this was indeed a question. And yet it was no small thing to admit yet another handle to his already buzzing portfolio of patronymics. Nevertheless he went so far at this point as to take a kiss on the forehead.

McCorkle went on: "I gave myself up for dead...

"Here I am trying to keep it pure for philosophy. But she's only keeping it pure for Vasselina. Through her I get wholesale protection from the come-ons of radical homosexuals. She was told that an unnamed queer was the source of my 'obsession' with philosophy. She intends to destroy him!

"I thought I could laugh her off. If she sailed to Piraeus, I'd fly to Trieste. When she popped up in Trieste, I'd take a night freighter to Izmir.

"But she gets there first! Izmir! All I have to do is take the Mercedes twenty miles to the dam at West Hinnstead, and she's there before me. There on the far bank in the turbine spray, waving like a maniac. 'Don't jump, don't jump!' And to that bank the road is seventy miles, and here is a woman who can't drive a grocery cart without a chauffeur and a cicerone.

"At Union Station there's a crew in her pay. Transportation stops when I show my face on a platform. When they're running again there's a private dick in every third seat and round about West Poolesville who comes swinging down from her roomette but Vasselina, not even to see McCorkle—fag-hunting down the line, packing her 38's in a basket of fried chicken.

"And Greyhound shuts down when I show. That leaves planes. Two springs past I had a phonecall relating to Yevlenkovich from Pensacola and took the next flight to Saskatoon. Now Vasselina is six feet tall, she lost sixty percent of her hearing and three toes riding the central laundry dryer at Lackland Air Force Base on a dare, and she has a glass eye, but when the stewardesses, six of them, trailed out of the cockpit, she, Vasselina, was a stewardess. And a very good stewardess she was! Such is the power of money, Yevlenkovich, in this rotten age." Hands to his temples, he leaned on the balustrade. "The tedium got to me, the tedium of trying to think of my own philosophical nonentity, meanwhile fighting an opposing opinion on the subject from an even greater nonentity at every pillar and post, and finally to use my last vacuole of philosophy trying in vain to hide from this nonentity, who gets where I'm going before I've even decided to go there, by running my past fugues and calendar aberrations through her family computer.

"Once I almost caught up with the fugacious Yevlenkovich. That boy scout in Saskatoon! I see you understand me. You left the youngblood's telephone number in a match pack in

Pensacola. But she headed me off on the landing ramp.

"Still it moved me to go on. I thought of Babaeski. Not to find you—but barring your presence to free up the conduit again for philosophy. This time I confessed to Vasselina before-hand. I begged her to let me go unmolested. She reluctantly agreed. Last Ground Hog day I sailed for Trieste...

"The new railroad goes through the barley fields where the platoon always camped west of town. The camp—gone, not a tent pole. A thrush sang out of the blackthorn thicket. Spring was breaking in Thrace, it was the eve of barley sowing. The western hillsides were sprayed with snow one morning, with anemones the next. Two red mules stood in the pine trees, pricking their ears toward Anatolia.

"I was in time for the festival. Shrove Tuesday the proces-sion marched to the churchyard at dawn. First came the village stud, the son of old Gheorghios, with a black rubber prick two feet long slung over his shoulder, stitched from old tire tubes. Some GI had sold him a Groucho nose and specs from the base PX in Istanbul. And a pair of regulation Gene 'Big Daddy' Lipscomb shoulder pads. Over that was a goatskin trailing half the flies in Macedonia. He stopped at a shack and yanked his bride out the front door on strings of bells—another big yokel, rice-powdered and rouged, in a yellow wig, bazooms stuffed with goosedown, and combat boots which he landed in Gheorghios's ass whenever the bridegroom got a step ahead. The 'wedding' popped out of doorways and courtyards, throw-ing meat, wine, bedstraw into the wagon. Little boys in short pants ran behind it with candles stuck in a bowl of barley.

"They saw her first. 'Babo, babo, babo!' I looked around and there she was, the old grandmother hooker pedalling through the crowd on her old Hercules with a baby on her arm, black stockings pumping a yard apart. 'Babo, babo, babo!' I ran after her too. Then the wind blows a gust, her hat sails down the street and there under that cone of veils is Vasselina." Shipoff laughed, and McCorkle slumped down on the railing. "Rotten money! The real *babo* was down at the local ginmill, drunk as a skunk. She hadn't seen so much money since Mustafa Kemal's irregulars rampaged the Edirne brothels in 1913.

"Vasselina nursing the babe, blessing the dung, terrorizing the bachelors, dropping seed—I left. The festival went on, no one else seemed to care. But I was glad to come home and be a nothing, a putz, a penis. I took this." And his beautiful arm (for he really was beautiful, monstrously luminous of face and limb and no more a part of the casual human landscape than a spotted ruby amanita toadstool or a gecko) stretched down towards the Arslevering pueblo shimmering in a wheel of green grass, cattails and footbridges.

"Might I point out," Shipoff said, "that if you had the Arslevering heiress on your side, you could ship half of Thrace to Little Athens, with change left over. She could hang red mules from the hornbeam grove if she took a fancy."

"No, she took the heart right out of it," said McCorkle. "Now if you had been here! Vassily Yevlenkovich, where the hell were you!

"I know what I am. I'm the type women tear apart on bush league ballfields every 4th of July in spontaneous collective intrauterine paroxysms. The National Guard never gets there in time for that poor jack. When five ladies and I face each other across a closed elevator I know how a pudding feels when it steams on the table. Hot but not hot enough!

"And except for my philosophy, or rather your philo-sophy—"

"Don't blame me," Shipoff said. "I like you as pudding. I prefer you as pudding."

"—except for philosophy, this...magnetism...is all I have."

"*Jawohl*," Shipoff said, "in truth is hope."

"Therefore I keep to well-lighted streets, I stay at Little Athens. I try to survive in one piece for the flow of philosophy. *My reel Takes the enTire Terror—*"

"*Recoil* Takes, recoil, recoil." Shipoff smiled indulgently at this reverent misquotation of the first Shipovian axiom.

It was a mistake. McCorkle went berserk: "Long Beach!

Tampico! Bereşna! Pensacola! Saratoga! Denver! Santiago! Shenandoah Downs! Where were you?" He seized Shipoff by the same collar that had subsided from Vasselina's manhandling, but quickly let him go. "Where were you on May 21st? Only Vassily Yevlenkovich could have stopped me from actually marrying this buzzard."

Now Shipoff stopped laughing, reached for McCorkle's shoulders and said with real emotion: "Then you are actually married to Madame Arslevering, my beloved and long straying Michael O'Fleer McCorkle." My beloved and long straying two-five-0 million dollars—the Depot was on!

"So you are not Shipoff but Vassily Alexis Yevlenkovich, who taught me to see by 'flattening the whiny and misery-glazed nose bulb,' as you called it—"

Shipoff snorted. It was plain, earnest lector, he hated this fellow.

"—the misery-glazed nose bulb on the podzols of the physical world, including the philosopher's asshole. You buggered me in Babaeski, blew me in a bathhouse in Äesme on Liberation Day, strongarmed my passport and a voucher for two years' pay and pushed me out of the bathhouse stark naked, with a gangbang of drunken housewives coming over the hill—"

There was a troubled silence as the magnitude of this crime shuddered in resurrection.

"*TAKEN: the enTire Terror,*" sang out Shipoff finally for he was no chicken.

"Taken, Taken," cried McCorkle. "A small price!"

They embraced like muzhiks.

"And here I am married, a putz, ruined!"

"I am Yevlenkovich, I am he."

"Even my name—cancelled."

"Arslevering will do." Shipoff patted his cheek. "And now down to business."

"Good," said McCorkle. "Everything is easy with Yevlenkovich here. I see what I have to do. She can spend the whole shitload on lawyers, I don't care. It's over! Again Yevlenkovich has come to McCorkle. She can keep it all, over the price of two railway berths to Edirne…"

The Depot was off. I saw those coils reverse in a massive hindthought.

"You must live with the woman Arslevering."

They stared at each other.

"I like you, McCorkle. But Babaeski is a sidetrip in no way convenient to my operations in the city-solo."

"Shipoff!" said McCorkle. "In ten years beating around the country after Yevlenkovich, his name popped up on a lot of bad paper. Perhaps you remember Altoona? a small drive-in folded? a depraved night manager named Gene? Or that little Baptist Teachers' College down a lane in Purval, Indiana. In Spokane your bad checks wrecked an orphanage and three pizza parlors! In penance the D.A., a personal friend of yours, wiped his ass with them for two months. Then Yevlenkovich may also recall—"

"Not Yevlenkovich," Shipoff said, "SHIPOFF, as in shape up or? Allow me to present to you my present project. In the season to come Babaeski will be to your final development as the old glider creaking on the front stoop was to the *poecile stoa* itself. So clean up your act for philosophy!"

McCorkle stood shaking.

"Well, think it over." And the master walked off at a leisurely clip toward Little Athens.

"A quarter billion," I lamented, as we looked around for the doctor.

"I'm not sure I need him, starboy," Shipoff muttered. "If he would leave Vasselina for me, then maybe all I need is her. As if I could tie on that caseload of Neostoical schizophrenia for a mere two hundred million without at least trying."

We found the doctor at the speakers' table behind the buffet, dipping scampi in sauce marinara, his left elbow lost in a mountain of chewed-off tails. One of the wasted old socialites that made up his entourage was tucking a clean bib over the filthy one already in his collar. "All right, Letty," he said as he saw us coming, "that's enough, be off." He smiled up wearily through smears of sauce. "*Fech!* self-indulgence. So what! Have some." But he had almost finished them.

O I was a Grecian braggadocio

We looked up in astonishment. For it was not Shipoff who sang from the platform, but a countertenor of pure and unearthly timber.

"Well, as I live an breathe," I said—

"Strike me blind," Shipoff murmured—

"Or I'm a born fool," said the doctor.

Chaspel Luckenkamp sang from the lectern, more bird than man.

VIII

Woman

"Surely a lector with no chippie is a starless vassal, a dog without a sail." So ruled Shipoff during a hypnotic blackout born of two pilfered fifths of the Arslevering's Pernod cast on twice that amount of high season oysters—it was New Year's Day.

This crackle surprised me from the old prop of itinerant pederasty. Still, howsoever rolled in the mangles of alcoholic aphasia, it gave me pause. A woman then. To find a woman: easy enough on the face of it, yes, and yet many the thyrsus bearers, few the bacchoi.

The field was not a crowded one. There were by now four women at the Depot, and these were irrevocably divided into two parties: the Vive Annie Analarge faction, which consisted of Annie herself, and the Topical Tropists' Anti-Annie Analarge League, which consisted of the remaining three ladies.

This trio, united under the gavel of Yeeza Ames, were themselves the female remnant of a group of aging and by now crusty novices, all of independent means, that had been following Dr. Analarge around for years. In spite of its relief from the worry of *machen a leben*, this group believed in work and, with their arrival, almost overnight a redistribution of menial labor took place at the Depot, beyond Shipoff's control and beyond his inclination to control. Suddenly there was a cafe-lounge

60

and a secretarial installation. They even brought with them the easels and duplicating equipment with which they had done the doctor's publicity in former years.

As a young plastic surgeon, educated in Salonika, Athens and Big Yolk, fresh from a Paris studio, Dr. Analarge had evinced a skill in classical facial reformation that augured to raise cosmetic surgery to the level of a humane discipline. His faces at that time were characterized by a profound simplicity and what was called, between eyebrows and jaw, "a pool of Olympian calm." It was at this time that a modest court began dogging the doctor around the country. In spite of his addiction to solitude, the doctor liked presiding in a coterie. And so reluctantly, after a number of years, he succumbed to pressure and did their faces one after the other.

Unhappily by this time the doctor's chronic derangement had already made incipient inroads. With them cropped up a new tendency toward abstraction and eccentricity in faces, with swiftly succeeding phases: for instance, Bionergic, neo-Pythagorean, "Mass-Broadcasting."

There were between the three ladies of the Anti-Annie Analarge League not only the powerful bonds of long comradeship behind the doctor and the possession of a common foe in his daughter, but also those of sisters-in-face, all three having been "done" in the doctor's Floricomous phase. Their present faces, best described as craggy, ended in hair that grew naturally into festive floral arrangements and wreaths. They were not unattractive. However, age was overtaking them, and by now the doctor had given up the remedial art in favor of his researches into the Inexpressible.

This common doom increased their rabidity towards the doctor's daughter, whose porcelain cheeks the doctor would never have had to practice upon. To complain about her arrogance the Anti-Annie Analarge League, known as AUNTY, met on alternate afternoons and evenings in the northwest waiting room that had become the Depot duplicating department, and which was run by AUNTY president Yeeza Ames in her civilian manifestation. Owing to Shipoff's aversion to putting anything in writing, this was a very part-time job. Therefore most of the time the ladies camped in semi-darkness amid slotted cubes of gray steel, idle rollers, black rubber mats and paper bins, awaiting inspiration. As defined in their charter, their purposes, when not strictly assassinatory, were charitable, not only for the purpose of obtaining cheap postal rates and other approbatory perquisites, but also for the thrill of running at least one of the shows at the Depot, albeit (geologically speaking) the lowest of the low, namely, the bughouse.

Before hibernation caught on in Big Yolk, we stowed our mad in the Pit, the bottom-most shaft where no tracks had ever been laid, later called the Hibernaculum. Relative to the upstairs population, the Pit did a flourishing business from an early date, since the pressures of education under the lectromagnate were great and, with one of the founders, namely Dr. Analarge, himself a chronic, a brief course of madness bore no stigma.

It happened that sole access to the Pit was via the northwest tunnel, the duplicating department. And so, willy or nilly, in a matter of weeks, AUNTY ran the Pit. There were standard rumors of atrocities but so long as the mad, such as they were, came straggling back upstairs again in about a fortnight, Shipoff left AUNTY to run it as they pleased.

No doubt it was necessary for AUNTY to console its thwarted femininity with an official grip on the shaft as strenuous as Annie's unofficial one upstairs. For on the other side of the hole Dr. Analarge jumped for his little Annie, Leftwich Proctor and Lambert Cauley, novice lectors, quivered at her approach, Alto Grizzard (of the doctor's band) kept back nothing from her, not even his baldness remedy, and even Shipoff, his mouth corners curling with unsaid sarcasms, his eye corners graven with acid repartee, nevertheless stepped aside for her at Depot functions, applauded her solos crisply, and acknowledged her "formidable" and "perfect" whenever a guest was fool enough to press him on the question.

To return to the Vive Annie Analarge faction. To say that Fraulein Analarge comprised a counteroffensive bloc in one body is no mere rhetorical gerrymander. In her free time, which was sundry and prodigious, when she was not picking locks in outlying Big Yolk for a surety in old age and time of war, cooking up hair oil by Grizzard's English formula, or strolling the Sumpsky Prospect with the doctor, she was composing verse satires on the ladies of the opposing camp, of which the following is a typical number:

> When Shipoff ships them to the freezer
> the Depot loonies bow to Caesar
> in the shape of AUNTY *Yeezer*.
> She soon shows them how to pleaser.
>
> As for the other AUNTY dames,
> let us judge them by their *Ames*.
> Chrust help our ears! they're full of names
> laid on her by the nuts she tames.
>
> Foul temptations crowd the head
> of her who seeks but honest bread
> in workaday from rise to bed
> to get her soul, not stomach fed.
>
> For her the devil list to hunt.
> He hopes to hear her stomach grunt,
> but Yeeza is above that stunt—
> she takes temptation up the c***.
>
> Tho' in the bughouse fore and aft
> he opes his toothy jaw in craft,
> lets burger odors work his graft
> and french fries from his gullet waft
>
> To hocus AUNTY, good or not,
> Why, she stays lean as any pole—
> she takes his hot air up her h***.
>
> O vice a little, vice a lot,
> vice untied th' umbilical knot
> and vice ties on the parting shot.
>
> He dangles meat but has no luck.
> To hell with food—she'd rather f***.
>
> —*Fanny*

63

Such were the broadsides that flapped, on dew-glazed mornings, in pastel hues from every aspen on the Sumpsky Prospect. Crunching up and down the walk on their daily business, AUNTY would take in these rags all day with frozen smiles. Then at dark, their weird cries frissoned the air as they ran from tree to tree...

Before I rolled my shopping cart onto this battlefield, I took to mind the bargain rate to be had from a lady likewise in the market. Was she in hot water? On the rebound? Down and out? Over the hump? On her beam ends? I would be interested. But there were other considerations.

For instance all three ladies of AUNTY were over the hump, and having all been conceived in Doctor Analarge's Floricomous period, they bore a strong resemblance to one another. How to choose between them?

Then I confess I was not wholly unsusceptible to the begonia complexion, the wide blue eyes, perfect little breasts and golden hair of Fraulein Analarge, although the mountain of tight curls on her already near six feet of height was rather overwhelming. Moreover Annie was surely in need in turn—in the classic debt of blood and vengeance. Didn't the sides stand at one to three?

I offered my services to Fraulein Analarge.

I managed to forget that AUNTY was possessed of the revenge factor triple strength. And now I know well enough that where one stands against three, odds on that the bitch in question is equal to three and three more of like stature. Not even the memory of Leftwich Proctor bobbing in her décolletage at the doctor's dinner-concert, with her good will, was enough to turn me aside at the time, not to mention the dreadful grin with which she received my proposition...

Ah well, let's get on with it.

Without fanfare, Annie took me into her camp. It was almost as if she had been expecting me, for there was a neat little desk in the corner of her office with ledger paper and sharpened pencils, a green visor hung up on a peg, a frame for the daily agenda, and, I couldn't help noticing, a padlock for the outer door, to help my concentration. There was even a sheet tacked over the sofa to prevent my cooping on the job. I had hardly opened my mouth, in short, before I was committed to so many hours a day. She did supply cigars.

Soon the clean lack of brother partisans to her cause became painfully conspicuous to me. What was the reason for this, when the Fraulein was so popular? I confronted Lambert Cauley on the subject in the new lector's lounge. Such an easy way to get a foot in her door. Whey didn't he drop up and volunteer? For of all her admirers, none was more in need of a hand or a foot of some kind than Cauley. Slothful, milk-fat, pimply, only the eighth part of an Arslevering in his veins and his wire to the Big Yolk theater district bartenders' grapevine got him by Shipoff, as a rule so favorably disposed to young men, much less past the arachnid scrutiny of Fraulein Analarge.

"A foot in the door," I pointed out.

"No shot!"

"Why not?"

"Prudence, my man."

"Prudence?—poo," I said. "What is prudence?"

"Prudence is three rich, ugly old maids with a broom closet full of Molotov cocktails at their disposal. And a looney bin! And all the duplicating equipment…"

I waved this by. "Think of the thanks you'd get—"

"Thanks!" He snorted in my face. "Remember Reddick? The secretary the doctor came in with? Poor chump! The doctor set him up like that, to 'go help Annie.' She put him to work on her books. He balanced her swag! He could have got ten years. Thanks? If he made a mistake she put the squeeze on his own pocket. He had to keep a little roster of her boyfriends, active and inactive, income, credit ratings, family connections… Do you know what she did, actually?" He smacked his glass down on the counter; he was drinking, as always, orange phosphate for his complexion. "She chained him to her book!"

"What was that?"

65

"CHAINED, chained. I swear to my god! It was only a little book, but it was degrading, hanging off his wrist everywhere he went for months. She tried to make him sign in and out but there he drew the line. And when she went dancing with Proctor he held her coat at the door—with the other hand. That's the kind of thanks he got. How's that for thanks?"

I shoved my left hand deeper into my topcoat pocket. It was true the book wasn't heavy, but the little chain bit. "No wonder he quit. Where did he end up, that Reddick?"

"Quit! He got sacked. It seems Fraulein A. told papa that his attentions were getting a little more enthusiastic than the job required..."

"So?"

"O he was ready to go! He went begging for a job on his knees from the Theater of the People of Barney Street, Big Yolk. A seasoned concertmeister, a junior diplomat and a Texan! But he's happy, he says, peddling wine at tree festivals."

IX
Vasselina

"Shipoff's Topical Tropists" snared a few halloos as a coming thing in the journals of sporting Big Yolk by the last snow of the first season, a St. John Chrysotom's day flooey of the meagrest description. The Arslevering money was now percolating in, a footgallon here, a footgallon there. What was obstructing an unbroken transfusion of funds from that vessel to this was the pure cantankerousness of Mrs. Arslevering. In spite of the doctor's influence, and though still strictly married according to Shipoff's command, Vasselina had detected the effects of a rival on her husband McCorkle, and reacted with a violence that made Shipoff up his daily alcohol intake by half for the rest of the winter. To wit: once so free with the ready, she became, overnight, tighter than the bark on a beech tree.

Crucial though it was to ward off open fire between the Arslevering spouses, still Shipoff saw fit to let Vasselina know that it was he, Sergei Shipoff, who had power to throw off Michael's gait, blow his tennis game, and lure his feet grotesquely onto those of his dancing partners. To effect all this, Shipoff had only to transit the Arslevering pueblo like a malevolent planet. Lest Vasselina cherish any doubts, the master would take up a cheroot and lean in the doorway staring at McCorkle, whereupon in a few minutes Michael would run to the bathroom and stick his finger down his throat, the better to "clear the conduit for philosophy." Even when Shipoff was off the premises there were signs. Vasselina divined a gentle bend in the random hard-ons that afflicted McCorkle as he lay on his butt in her four-poster, smoking hashish and reading the evening paper. It was westward as the crow flies, towards the Depot.

Not that Vasselina cared about the inclination, so long as he had the erection, and so long as it lasted, now and then, long enough to get clamped in the hole for which nature inspired it. In this hope she had a powerful ally unbeknownst to her: Shipoff. He ordered McCorkle to service the Arslevering heiress nightly if possible, triweekly without fail; for what she had could be threatened with removal, whereas what a woman has not, how can anyone take this away from her?

It was no use. Nor was it any use to threaten Vasselina with deprivation, since to make their unions even slightly less frequent than they had been before Shipoff came on the scene would have been, alas! to sow them across the connubial tundra at expanses vast to the point of invisibility, Siberian distances, featureless wastes indeed. No, instead it came to be Shipoff's concern to make sure that Vasselina did not forget the pangs and pleasures of married life altogether.

On both sides, maneuvering dragged on. Shipoff was afraid to allow McCorkle out of Little Athens for even a night, for fear Vasselina might actually crack the domestic habit. Vasselina, for her part, installed overnight a *quid pro quo* system of household economics, with the *quids* new grand notes and the *quos* long drills, before bedtime, on general questions like: where had he been all day? From breakfast to 9:10, for example? Nine ten to nine twenty? Nine twenty to nine thirty? and so on. If he stuck it out as far as the postprandial hours which Shipoff insisted he spend in the bosom of his family, then McCorkle got the grand note, and next day we bought groceries, paid the Depot telephone bill, sent flyers to press, etc. But McCorkle was weak. "He never could take it," said the master.

It would have been grossly unlike the Shipoff who meant to

be leading lectromagnate of Big Yolk and the Americas, to settle for long on a coil so aggravatedly conditional. He soon took a new track.

One morning in February he called me to him. His toady found me in Annie's apartment, tabulating hair oil receipts, sweating and cursing. What had possessed me to go to the woman? Lector or not, chippie or not, I had to get out of her closet.

At first I thought I was free. Shipoff lay among pillows and blankets on his favorite bench in the Grand Concourse. "Squeeze on, starboy, there's room," he said, moving over as though there were no less between us than that first day under the horse chestnut. "Chrust! I like those thingabobs more every minute, there's a future in them and they're new as a new tooth!" Touching my ear bobs, he made the sound that plaza shoppers emit when peering into baby carriages.

Behind these dotings, the reasoning was not obscure. Remember the pinheaded Luckenkamp! who no sooner showed his face at Little Athens than he landed feet first in the big time, at no cost to himself and miles in excess of Shipoff's most extravagant prophecies for him. Shipoff was agonized by the miscalculations that had caused him to let the little D.D. slip through his coils to stardom in the city-solo. So what if Shipoff had really expected the citizens-solo to bounce Chaspel out on his ear, an ear small even for the head that transported it? And if now they were saying that Chaspel Luckenkamp had the voice of his age, what then? Let the simple believe it was what came out of his mouth that had made him. Shipoff knew it was that head! Now more than ever he was obsessed with the power of abnormal surfaces, pregnant with mass recoils.

So he never missed a chance to cream over my ear wattles, spoon-feeding my doubts on prochromosomal bull-guano of his own devising. As now: "You know, they're like turkey wattles, Hughby, that's what they are! Jawbones, they remind me of Thanksgiving dinner at home with the family."

Dallying this morning with my ear bobs, Shipoff's eye fell on my left hand, which was crammed under my lapel deep in an imaginary waistcoat. He suddenly jerked it out like a carrot.

The roster book of Annie's cash romances dangled sordidly between us.

Shipoff gave me a look of bottomless disgust and flipped through it in silence, snoring here, scowling there, jotting a name and phone number down from time to time on the back of the bench. Then he jerked the little book off its chain and threaded it through the grate of the kerosene stove at his feet.

"Business first: mine first of the first."

"That's fine with me," I replied.

"O it is," he sneered. "What do you mean by feeding yourself to that Analarge bitch in the first place? I won't bail you out either, Hughby. Why should I? She'll take care of you, she'll serve you up proper, trussed up and carved on her father's sideboard. Goodbye, starboy, for you the star is over..."

"Surely a lector with no chippie is a starless vassal, a dog without a sail," I said. "You didn't say which chippie."

"Did you ask?" said Shipoff. "When entreated to run his life by any of my young scholars did you ever know me to turn him down? No, no, Hughby, even I wouldn't palm you off on a vicious greedy cunt like that. I think more of you! Believe me, starboy. For you?" He lay back in his featherbed, one gloved hand in the air, conjuring bareassed nymphs from the skylight. "First of all, a highborn woman, a rich and generous woman, to recoup your past losses and, er, pad the small shocks to come. A woman with a taste for the new and the rare, who will cherish your special appendages. A strong woman! A woman with balls, a daredevil! But respectable—preferably a married woman, since the lector ties no knots. A woman of muscle and municipal reputation..."

I started for the upramp.

"Of prowess and positive if highly variable appearance..."

"Forget it," I said. "That woman is dangerous. McCorkle told me all about her. She breaks bones!"

"Woo the Arslevering woman, Hughby—"

70

"Roll on, boss, I'm not your Texarkana bunboy," I said. "I'd never get back to the Depot—admit it! My training, kaput! You're just trying to get rid of me!"

"Wait, wait. Woo her, not win her, starboy, just wheedle, fuck around, ply the trade, play, tittle, make naughty-naughty— that's all. She loves her husband. He loves me! She's got something on him—I need something on her. Just a little something! Come on, Hughby, keep it in mind: rational beings exist for one another, you for me, me for you.

"Think about it for a week, but don't pass it up. My stars! Where's your old ambition, Hughby? Slam gone?"

*** MY AMBITION ***
Q: Where was it?
"Or was it I that went?"

Well asked! Timeout for a capsule review of the tropos.

INTERPRETATION OF THE FOREGOING INTERVIEW

As I chugged towards Shipoff's ambush at the next switch-siding, he wound up the Vasselina Arslevering courtship topos to sling it on me qua mailbag. Earnest lector, as you just saw, in broad daylight and high confidence he did this, such was his presumption on my usual good will.

However, my Ambition did a back flip at the mere sight of him. It was unpremeditated. By St. Cornwallis, if you could have found me you could have stirred me with a spoon.

As it happened I somersaulted into space without rails or intersections, and for a while I drifted trackless and free under the starpoints of Stanley and Speke, and through the dark nights of box-car tourists and flophouse bums.

I looked over my shoulder. A silvery tape looped off behind me, gleaming in the starlight. My track, I suppose? It looked like silver. Closer inspection revealed it was shit. I squinted: down at his end Shipoff snored on his divan, his arms thrown over the sides.

Homeless again. Then where to? To say I was sick of man-fresser Annie and the lectromagnate Shipoff, yet ad-

71

mit they were "of the masterful," was only to take on
worthy enemies. It is the same to dog the song and dance
of a worthy enemy as to get a master by heart, even the
same. More desperate yet! For now you're at war to get his
10-wheeler rote ditty under your skull without catching a
slug in the bald spot. Or else he disappears with what he
knows…

To war then.

Education as war. If I had a dollar for every stop I would
make to stoke up my topos beside a master's! The fact is, I
lost a dollar every time, give or take 15 cents, and a mercy
it is, by the bones of St. Cornwallis at Ghazipur. By the
parliamentary click of the House-Father's bones, derailed
there between rose fields and opium barns where the
Ganges gurgles through the perfume distilleries—for that
too I thank Providence.

I was lucky in my enemies. What did I need so much as
my enemies, after all. And what is love, but incontinent
need performing hair-raising acts of levitation on the whirl-
wind? Who can love his enemies like the chump with a
mania for war, like myself, Shamp, I mean. Well, I loved
them. The hours I spent under Brakeknot, Shipoff, Analarge,
Tapsvine, glad to cadge fugitive whiffs of the great men's
feet! Would they had toppled off their trestles! But I had to
wait till their engines had rolled down the hill and gone
before I knew what they left me: only a faint coolness where
the sun was interrupted.

I loved them, like father brother & son I loved them.

But forgive them? Never. My brain is incurably corru-
gated with their tracks, like a boxtop.

Compare even Chaspel Luckenkamp's case to mine,
before he got rich and famous, even before he picked
Shipoff and me up in Bulimy County and set his course on
Big Yolk. Always he puttered over his own little track,
disregarding a lynch threat here and a bunco steerer there.
He had a customized calling that revolved painlessly between flocks anthropoid and gallinaceous, between inten-
tions salvational and carnivorous, on the strength of the
constant participation and encouragement of Chaspel
Luckenkamp, D.D., himself, solo, dead center. The world
rolled out from his ignorant pinpoint full of holes it is true,
great craters where whole tropics and hemispheres had

fallen out, but he knew where he was with respect to the general item—right in the middle, wherever he stepped off his running board.

But me? Let me put it, that upon waking as before sleeping, when walking up the Prospect, picking my way from the Depot across fields of stubble to the pay phone at Blumberg's Truckers' PURE & Oasis, watching the semis pull up in West Poolesville on a summer afternoon, hearing in their huge sniffs the blurred transit of 2000 miles of hills and sand, loamy rivers and wastes,

When I would pass the West Poolesville dime store on a summer day, floating down the channel of mica and Marlboro butts, blinded by the sidewalk, cut loose in the mortal starlight, afloat facedown and eyes ajar in the fatal tank of day,

Whenever I ceased for that instant to compare myself to my mighty models, to peruse the tracks and recoils of the masters, to dog their effortless pedesis, or to feed the pigeons, I was saying:

What is this place to me? this point which takes all points? this point in which all points rest?

Then I might cry for my home, or feed the pigeons.

Pigeons…? Where were my pigeons?

What was holding me up out here? A ribbon of shit! By Chrust, in an instant I would be smashed to atoms. Stuffing my necktie in my mouth to keep from twittering, holding my breath so as not to alert the elements, I climbed hand under hand down the beanstalk of my Ambition.

———

X

The Sham Topos

I had one more day to give Shipoff my yea or nay on court-
ing Vasselina. Then a still more critical hole in the Depot
operations yawned to be plugged. Again I thought I was free.

Though the Arslevering subsidy flowed in fitfully if at all,
across the Sump in Big Yolk rumors multiplied as usual. People
thought we were rich, since the Arsleverings had never before
paid attention to a cultus without rolling it in wads of instant
capital. Accordingly the Depot buzzed towards fashionability,
as flies over river mud grow thicker in a dry spell. And now the
Depot began to draw bands of the curious—drifters, spongers,
slackers, floaters, supplicants, and finally volunteers.

Shipoff and Dr. Analarge soon collided on this point.

Shipoff was well pleased at the influx of potential whatevers,
and desired to impress them still more with the solidity of his
operation by providing a tour of the permanent, standing,
aboveground erections appertaining to the Depot, of which
there was at that time only one: namely, the prefabricated
home and laboratory of Analarge and daughter, provided to
himself, by himself, for his own greater comfort and felicity.

Moreover, the doctor had secured to his bosom the exclusive
dispensation, at Shipoff's Topical Tropists, of weekends off.

He was therefore annoyed at the intrusion of Shipovian
maneuvers into his establishment on Saturdays, and installed,

after the first onslaught, an enormous gargoyled padlock on the vestibule door, which he declined to remove until the following ground rules were laid:

1. There would be one tour of his quarters per Saturday, at exactly 2 p.m., and he, Analarge, would lead it.

2. He would have first crack at every prospective volunteer, and the methods of initiation be left to his discretion.

3. He would be henceforth, and forthwith, provided with a *sham topos,* animal vegetable or mineral, by the Saturday, to set up as a morphological "Exhibit" wherewith to fend off, by distraction, jarring extraneous questions from the mob, with respect to his real researches into the Inexpressible.

When the question of a sham was aired at a Depot assembly, Lambert Cauley said: "I nominate Hughbury *Sham.*" Boundless merriment—I daresay I smiled myself.

Then Shipoff said: "Those ear plummets: they're four weeks old today."

(This was before, but not long before, Shipoff's unctuous blandishments of these tumors began to wear thin, and they came to mortify me to the point of mania.)

Analarge: "*Nota:* they outsize the basal lobe one and a half times. A secondary sexual character that's a junk jewelry phenocopy. He's the logical choice."

As the laughter had not yet subsided from Cauley's pun, I stood up in confusion. Shipoff pulled me down. "Good boy! They look fine!"

"He'll do," said the doctor.

"He's yours," said Shipoff.

I left the meeting with my head whizzing like the Big Yolk Beltway. Vasselina had been dropped at an overpass. But here was the doctor. As for Annie and me ever tearing up the road together, what a laugh. Too late to use papa for that. But gracefully to yield up my surfaces once a Saturday might have other interests, other returns. A fair chance, for one, to get close to the doctor himself, who since Reddick was sacked was in need of an assistant.

Now, I liked Dr. Analarge, his solitude, his island force. He had the presence of an old oak in a short stand of pine scrub. And I was sick of Shipoff—"Turkey diddley-watts... Thanksgiving at home with all the little Shipoffs..." Jawbones!

So my recoil from the master was delivered to the doctor, Shipoff's gift. "He's yours." The snake, he thought of everything.

Now closed in the blackest days of my nymphalid existence.

For four or five Saturdays running, the tour was a slapdash affair, dispersed by 2:15, in which I as the draw nevertheless received only a summary gape and an occasional prod from the brazen. At 2 p.m. Analarge would take in a sore eyeful at the vestibule keyhole, sniff, climb up the loft ladder, roll it up behind him, hook it past the aperture, slide back down the pole, lock up his desk and cram exposed papers. At 2:05 he rolled me into the middle of the floor. Then lighting a Jamaican perfecto and sighing heavily, he sprang the latch.

During this period my projected alliance with the doctor moved along unspectacularly. First of all came a little note from him (in Annie's scrawl) bidding me understand that no excuse would be sufficient for presenting myself in his eyesight before 1:55 p.m. on any Saturday, nor later than 2:00, "dress unimportant." At 2:04 p.m. the doctor, who was a kindly man, voiced a few standard condolences between cigar blasts as he strapped me into his facial-surgical chair, idle since he had abandoned the art for the Inexpressible. I would then be released, one might almost say ejected, from the seat of duty at 2:15 flat.

On the verge of my sixth Saturday on show, however, at 2:00 p.m., Analarge rose from the keyhole and did not sniff, but rather lit his perfecto without further observances, and leaned thoughtfully against the panelling. "Hughbury, could you go for a little fiction...a connection, perpetrated by myself, ha-ha, between those pimento ear bobs of yours, *fech!* and your innocent tochos. A little self-indulgence—just for the afternoon. Will you play along?"

Play? I labored along! I was a wild-eyed flunkey, I could not pick and choose. He who says Let my dear hunkers off is an eye that hankers for green things, a tooth that hankers for soft things. The idea was in my mind that we were cohorts.

The tour went on as ever till 2:15, when herding the swine toward the exit the doctor tiptoed hastily to the back of a certain guest, gathered the slack of his departing trousers with one fist and pressed the door shut with the other.

The face of the visitor, which now turned whitely upon us, was remarkable for its lack of eyebrows. The disk that remained was a well-lit arena wherein shock and fatigue vied constantly for territory—it had been "done," I heard later, by the doctor in his "plain" period. Its owner shuffled down the lab until he reached the chair the greatest distance from me. There he sat down, twined his legs around each other, and lit a cigarette shakily.

Analarge, beaming, seized the facial-surgical chair by its chrome handles and wheeled me at a murderous rate down the room, stopping short at his guest's thinning hairline. His cigarette fell to the floor. Analarge kicked it away, and handed the fool a Perfecto #1. (He had yet to offer me a nickel stogy—depressing.) He then bent to loosen my straps, meanwhile nailing me with a glance calculated to send any private impulses I might have been developing crashing back to zero.

The doctor set me on my feet. "Now what do you think of this, Empory? I was thinking it would harrow all hell in Tulsa."

They were friends of a sort, Empory a fugitive from the little band the doctor still managed to draw after him in spite of his shifting afflictions and enthusiasms. Empory struggled to lift his eyes to me. As the waterclock in the loft warbled 2:30, his gaze reached my ears. He still cringed academically, but fatigue had won, the war was over.

"It was nerves—" Empory began.

The doctor waved it aside. He was in high spirits:

"No excuses, you're home, no?"

"I don't know, doc," said Empory, pointing at me. "What's with the freakshow? Are you trying to take me in?"

"What! *Gait*, do you think he was born wattled? Feel!" He clamped Empory's hand over ear wattle A. Empory's upper lip sprang toward his nostrils.

"Plasticine," he said faintly.

"Flesh!" said the doctor, slapping his rubber glove on my buttocks. "All it is, is modified toches. You know that's old hat. The advance here is bleeding in color. What would you call this tint? Big Yolk Raspberry?" He pulled ear wattle B toward the window light.

Empory said nothing.

Analarge wiped his opalescent brow. "Now look here! Take one of these. Now damn you, I said take it." His own small fingernails clamped firmly onto my left buttock. Empory reluctantly took the other. "So! What have you got, eh? I'll tell you! You have one Euclidean lifetime of woe just to figure out where one plane leaves off and the next begins even in this monochromatic bilge-ridden pad of a porklump you see before you." And he yanked my hospital gown to my waist.

Assistant or no assistant, the joy went out of it, as far as I was concerned. But before I could present my case, Dr. Analarge turned upon me:

"A propos of your privates, Hughbury, my daughter's been looking for you. Why don't you just whizzle those wattles, ho-ho, over to the subway and give her a tumble?"

Give her a tumble! This inexpressibly uncharacteristic advice from the doctor had a double intent:

(a) to get rid of me chop-chop, and

(b) to stagger his old friend and potential drone with a show of the open policy towards animal joys supposedly in vogue at the Depot.

Transparent though this ploy may appear to you, earnest lector, it was worth a try! I shucked the hospital dress, pulled on my drawers and started for the subway. But I dropped my comb in the laboratory vestibule, and crawling around on my hands and knees in search of it, I heard Analarge shout:

"My boils I am, my boils I am!—no retrograde, Lilly-livered illusionist ever, but ever traversed this vestibule, Empory Harfanger. It's a small outfit we have here, a little wort-cunning, a little stargazing, a little old style leechery: if you don't like it, rump it, but if you don't like it you don't get it."

There was no mistaking the coveted proposition. But what did Empory Harfanger have that I, Hughbury, lacked?

✧ ✧ ✧

In five minutes time I was sitting at my little desk in Annie's apartment, my palms cradling my forehead, my coat folded neatly in my lap. "Cauley!" I burst out again. "Cauley! Not Cauley!" For I had passed Lambert Cauley on the way out, his belt unbuckled, his chops curled up in an unmistakable grin. "Cauley!" I said once more. "Your dad..." No, the stupidity of that line of attack was too obvious. Hardly Shipovian Calculus on her Recoil, since, wrapped in a chrysalis of linens on the sofa, Annie had yet to acknowledge my presence. I fished for her recoil: "Throes of conscience, eh? Then why Cauley, considering that he gives you a pain, murders your afternoon, muddles your virtue, cankers your prospects..."

At last she chuckled from under the covers: "Because, *lieber* Hughber, he has even more greenbacks in his pocket per pocket than he has pimples on his chin per chin." And she expelled her slender head and uppers from the bedclothes. Her skin shone on a white morbid softness that begged to be split and spilled, if you could and would...

Rage. So the maggot rolled up in her puparium strictly to plug a horselaugh at my situation. Then the Cauley acneiform jawbone came to my mind, and Chrust help me, I laughed. "A pock well taken."

A natural chump! What Empory Harfanger had he had. As for me I went naked, waiting for the gaps to close in my customized education.

XI

S.C.O.R.

Education services time, ever laying its track in two directions—there and back. Thus the hard times get connected to
the soft, for the hindsight of collectors, enthusiasts, and boardwalk philosophers like myself.

In those days I had endless room for instruction. Shipoff had
made a few powerful points, but what were they to a loop-the-
loop like my tropos, little points made by one who knew where
he was going on the track of one not even sure he was going?

I was no longer starboy to the lectromagnate. There were
twenty starboys, and I was neither first nor last in magnitude: I
was "the turkey-wattled."

I had the benefit of Shipoff's expertise every morning all the
same, in his class in *Calculus On The Recoil*, which balanced
Doctor Analarge's p.m. ministrations *Toward the Inexpressible.*

It was Shipoff's chief joy that his three-week course in the
S.C.O.R. remained elective through the seasons, yet attracted
the enrollment of every novice lector to a man, and was even
infiltrated (a real victory) from time to time by spies from the
Theater of the People of Barney Street, Big Yolk.

But if registration was optional but perfect those first three
weeks by a spontaneous mass systole of the sophomoric will, I
can testify all the same that in weeks to follow this mitzvah was
reenacted carefully, under pressure of two devices:

1. The delivery of a powerful hint upon Shipoff's chief joy, to an influx of starboys still thrashing around in the thin broth of early ambition, in which kissable asses float like dumplings, and dumplings are manned like life rafts, and,

2. The distribution of the Syllabus (q.v.*) than which nothing could have been more misleading.

---

*SYLLABUS

THE SHIPOVIAN CALCULUS
—INSTANT—   *—THEORETICAL—*

Taught By The Founder
SERGEI SHIPOFF

Teaching, the Detection & Measurement, According to SHIPOFF, of the Conscious or Unconscious Contribution To Your Cause, of Your Personal, Animal, Vegetable, Mineral, Mechanical FOE.

"Taken, the enTire Terror is advanTageous."

A Course In
COURSE & RECOURSE IN COIL & RECOIL
CLASSICAL   *NIGHT-FLYING*

Sound Instruction In:

The Omnivore Of The Future
Theoretical Hibernation
Protracting The Totter
Marsupial Cataplexy Humanized
Genius In Negligence & Omission
Recent Refinements In The Retreat
Uses Of The Schmeer Pot
… and many more too numerous to mention.

The syllabus seemed to promise endless rafting down the lacy arteries of arcane combat strategy, in search of a mastery as replete as it was, by any other route, inaccessible. But the actual Calculus On the Recoil as taught by Shipoff was a one-lane track of the simplest. If the doctor's Inexpressible was a thought hard to pinpoint, Shipoff's Calculus, on the contrary, was a presence impossible to escape, at least if the lectromagnate were on the premises. For far from stinting the small fry, Shipoff, in the mercy of his coils, never tired of rising (or extending) to the occasion. He couldn't teach the S.C.O.R. without pulling it off continuously. Hence if it happened that a novice crossed the lectromagnate's threshold with a topos fit to his coils, he would have him for lunch. If a novice on the other hand got a toehold on a threshold not Shipoff's but its better, the lectromagnate switched thresholds so swiftly that even your own seemed cut to his butt and not yours: he would goose you from behind while you stood guard in your own vestibule.

"Recoil and endure," said the lectromagnate one week when the vodka was at the flood. "To recoil is to be author, publicist, dealer, impresario, hack, screw, butcher, baker, palmer, procurer, furrier, fueler, fowler, hooker, hocker, miller, wife, dragoman, thief, chauffeur, housefather, tin badge and board president of your own fate."

"Butcher your own fate and endure?" I asked recklessly. "Who would pay cash money for that lesson?"

"Any butcher, for example. In fact, Hughby, give me a first line for the topos: *The Butcher Auto-Butchered.*"

This was my luncheon invitation, the basic exercise.

I reflected a bit and came up with:

> *The executioner rose late…*

Shipoff pounded on the lectern. "Super-duper, gyroscopic." After a moment's meditation he pursued:

> *The executioner rose late.*
> *Starved for consent*
> *His old blade rent.*
>
> *But blessed with laud*
> *His rigors thawed.*
> *Thus fashion's rise was felling fate.*

Now it was my turn to applaud. A touching topos of the butcher who, abashed at acclaim, gratefully loses his grip on his hatchet, only to be recoiled from in turn, even from his own state of impulsive and charitable recoil.

O fame loved life!

(I took off)

His ax recoiled!
But minus knife
His fame was foiled.

Down down he fell …

All at once I saw something sadly fetching in the butcher's unterminated topple.

"The End," I stuck on.

"The End! You've left the little hit man in a passive tailspin," Shipoff said. "Let him out!"

"It's a new twist in the old multiple recoil yarn…"

"It wasn't the staleness of your topos that caused us to snore, Hughby, it was that Old Autobiographical Slow Drag in the hindparts."

"Now whatever in Chrust I am," I said, "I am not a butcher."

Shipoff shook his head. "You're gainsaying the lectromagnate. Now gentlemen, will you tell Mr. Shamp one infallible method that every novice lector commands of butchering his own fate?"

The class rumbled in unison: "Gainsaying the lectromagnate…"

"And now, Hughbury. The lectromagnate says you are *butcher*. You say you are not *butcher*. You contradict the lectromagnate, therefore you are *butcher* sure enough, out front and slam dead in the home coliseum, we see you very plain.

"And the gracefullest tropos for the little butcher in his decline is of course to excuse himself with his own hatchet.

Now scorned, he gave himself the prize:
The 'ex' of his master's ax man, dies."

"Check out just like that?" I said. "Hardly Shipovian…"

"We can't all be Shipoffs."

I jumped up. No matter how fast you shucked it there was a caterpillar in your corn, ear after green slickered ear, and that caterpillar was Shipoff. "O? Well, I protest the butcher's auto-butchery 'according to the S.C.O.R.' In my interpretation the sentimental butcher's commendable recoil from butchery is brutally butchered by the S.C.O.R. in the person of the founder, a far more steely-eyed butcher than the little butcher ever dreamed of. It's a frame-up. And the gentle butcher's big toe sliding dutifully over his ear and up the scaffold to slip the blade on his own guillotine is a case of other-butchery, that is, murder, in which one man's de-feet is another man's foison…"

"Tut! if the butcher takes it personally, he should recoil to the bughouse as fast as his mangled stubs can carry him." Shipoff turned to the class, pacing up and down. "The nerve of the butcher, making puns on my class time! All this is Protracting the Totter…it is vain. I could pardon the flummery in a sportsman, an amateur, a Chautauqua prophet for hire by the Sunday…

"But a practicing lector in the city-solo?

"Get back to scratch, Shamp, go play in the exhaust vent." He meant this literally: go to the fan, do instant S.C. on a mechanical opponent, by simple arithmetic on the gasps my sincere desire to recoil. I looked up at the giant flat fan blades metabolically frolicking in their fretwork indusium.

The bell rang. "Tomorrow: *Igneous Eructations, fact or fancy*," said the lectromagnate. "As for you, Shamp, go back to lesson three, clearing the clogged-up kitchen ventilator of surplus cafeteria crockery with a little eggbeater action of the metatarsals, after penetrating the exhaust tunnel on all fours. Tomorrow you put my socks in the dryer from the inside."

I decided I needed Dr. Analarge for a master.

XII

The Inexpressible

I believed that the doctor would show me all he saw, if only we found grounds to meet upon. Even before the Sham was set up, we were not short of intersections. He roared by me five or ten times a day in the fast mail habit of all the masters, but before I could whine *Take me*, he was gone.

I was attending his class in the Inexpressible, but far from fostering our transactions, it was the meatless fare of these symposia that first turned my tracks toward the Sham to get a good crack at the doctor, humble though the ambush. At least it transported my ass past the queue of featureless novices in his laboratory vestibule into the interior, on the model of the fly that buzzed over the wazirs prostrate in the anteroom to light on the caliph's nose, a felicitous conjunction of the Insignificant and Insignificating with the Compassionate and Compassionating, on the bulbous grounds of his boredom.

Though kind by nature, as a master the doctor was a caliph. The pose that he chose to strike before his dusts of students was such that you spent a long afternoon gazing up at his ankles, at his shinbones boiling in cloudlight through the roof and out of sight, so that from the kneecaps on up the doctor was a topos beyond mortal consideration. In return for his hubris and the colossal obscurities he peddled, Doctor Analarge was generally hated by novice lectors, on whose personalities he likewise declared war in his tropos "Toward the Inexpressible.'

His first lecture:

"Forget what you know. The considered life boils down in this class to Conventions, Concessions *and* Inexpressibles. *Concessions: really the median factor is nothing but semidigested convention, convention prior, but en route, to the crapper. For the House of Man is Convention. As shit to the garden, so concession to the house!—for it is pleasing to the eye of nature that the future of convention be manured continuously in her eyesight, yea that it be manured incessantly by the drek of disputations is pleasing to her eye.*

"Don't be misled, little children, the disputants are real, they're out for blood. They stand there face to face belching their proper names in each other's faces—but can a name be empty? Not by half!—one croaks and the other croaks back, be it only to fend off the killjoy of auscultation. But too late! Never mind the words: the heard is already conceded. From there to convention is no sooner said than..."

Second lecture:

"Let us now contemplate our experience in the present, in its inexpressible state, still foundering afloat the multiple bands of boomlay it is bound to mobilize in the home crasis. We see ourselves bob in the endoplasm of interior time, where past present and future are one, already forewarned and rebuked, each penitent nuclei in its own unicellular cesspool.

"This is the point, the point made all! The Inexpressible Point!

"But to speak? to speak is to abandon the point! For between two words is convention, the same old track, and what is this track in a man but a PERSONALITY?

"A PERSONALITY: *the Inexpressible reeled in and tanned for a volley ball. A varicosity of conventional tracks, overadaptational thrombosis, a congeries you might retch to find in the bottom of a bait can..."*

To thwart in each novice lector, for a minute a day if no more, the accumulation of a Personality—this was the doctor's aim. And every lector afflicted with a Personality, which was all of us, of course, not all at once, but all in good time, caught shit from the doctor accordingly: lab-swabbing and sock-washing details, afternoons "helping Annie" (but Shipoff put an end to that), plus the eternal assignment:

To avoid repeating the course, each novice was obliged to produce three Inexpressibles per six-week course for the doctor's approval, to be heard by the doctor on class time. Express the Inexpressible on class time? Nobody understood a word he was talking about! Nevertheless every two weeks the puling band filed into the laboratory block to be counted and kicked for good measure. Personality gave way to terror. The confusion was indeed Inexpressible. There was one ploy you could try to slip by the doctor: you could pop off with a general inquiry at just so many seconds from your turn as could be counted on two chicken hooks. If the doctor got interested, bully for you. If not, your Personality got his special attention.

I said: "I'm thinking of a topos, Doctor Analarge, wondering if it can survive experience as an Inexpressible Point, so rather than trundle blindly ahead, I'll ask you if it is one."

"And what might that be?" The doctor lifted his eyebrows, as wind lifts an oakbough.

"O, love, affection, nuptials, necking, butt-rubbing, crotch-sniffing, all that sort of topos."

Analarge blinked. "Tropos, tropos. Well, I know what you hear, but love isn't all that great, little pork, no, it ain't everything."

"Ahhh." I slid away from the lectern at the speed of sweat. Then I stopped. Love a tropos? just a convention, a hernia off the Inexpressible Point, a noose for the spirit strung between blabbering personalties? Love a tropos!

I turned, and just as I turned he turned. There was proof in the caliph's eye that the fly on his nose was not excusable.

"No, not even the *Balling of Fraulein Analarge* topos, little pork."

The balling of Fraulein Analarge!

"Come, come, nor can that topos be empty, little porkpie. Report!"

The doctor took me up by the buttonhole and waltzed me strenuously to the rear, where he bounced me off the slide projector. "*Fech!* Surely this is a matter whereanent silence can not be kept! Details, little pork."

I shrugged. "Doctor, a little mix-up of personalities, a passing tropos…"

"Little pork, it's the old tropos all right, but a big mix-up. My daughter Annie, you recall her"—he pinched my cheek—"is heavy with RUNT. She confided to *lieber* Papa—topos extraordinaire, you lucky pork—it's all yours! So let's have the whole story!"

"Mine!" I laughed. "Impossible."

"Impossible! O ho!" The doctor spat past my ear, a clam full of garlic, trained on the Arctic aurora. "Did you write the handbook? What gives you to say impossible, little porkpie? What do you know?"

"The classical…distinction, the obvious failure to…come together…"

The class tittered.

"A detail," said the doctor. "My daughter has method, she knows whereof she speaks!" He sank suddenly into one of the little wooden desks, his belly resting on the platform, his head in his hands. "She's a beautiful girl, who could resist her? Think of those little breast buds—so I've seen them—who hasn't."

It was true she exposed them at every pretext.

"Think of those nipples, those kissable, perfect coppers, embossed like the medallions of the Florentine Pompanozzi. Having read the fine print"—he turned to me again—"have the goodness, lucky boy, to share the info with a proud papa. What do they say? DUPLEX GLORIA, perhaps? or CRESCITE ET MULTIPLICAMINI, like two little states of Maryland?

"Well, what do they?" He socked me in the face.

"I'm innocent!" I said. "Anyway ask Shipoff—I can't help you—lectors never marry."

"Marry!" roared the doctor. "*Schmegegi!* The idea. Marry! You are crazy! *Rachmones*, what an inspiration. You and my daughter—may you break a leg for entertaining such a thought. That's it! In a pig's eye! Marry! I've heard everything…"

XIII

The Pit

Was I crazy? A tub of opinion, in a sea of transformation...

Nevertheless the doctor did not forget to send me a two-week pass to the bughouse, along with his wishes for my speedy reconstitution.

No, no, he was sincere, there was even a peaceable little note in his own hand for a change, excusing me from the Sham for two Saturdays, if I went down.

Down I went. As I have said, insanity was no great fall at the Depot: it was a part of nature, a state, nor can a state be empty but has its little graces, uses and abuses. A trip down the shaft without a pass from one of the masters ate up vacation days at a terrible rate. As for the passes, the longest expired in a fortnight.

In fact, two weeks was plenty. You will recall that AUNTY ran the Pit. A touch of gratuitous sadism notwithstanding, this was exemplary Shipovian Calculus On The Recoil. For if there was high volume lunacy upstairs at the Depot, there was likewise high turnover lunacy from the basement, with most of the mad streaming up from the Pit in a week, often shrieking with relief at the exit.

As for me it took a scant eight hours to make tracks—but then, AUNTY dosed me with special attention.

I showed my pass at the Depot duplicating department at

8 a.m. President Yeeza Ames sat up in her sleeping bag and, from under her battered floral coiffure, cast an eye on me by no means kind. I thought back to her winks, affable if grotesque, over our toast at the doctor's dinner concert. Perhaps she had had her bellyful of smooth-cheeked novices by now? Maybe she was just a crabby riser. Why should she hate me, Hughbury, in particular? Did she even know me?

"Well, what'll it be, Shamp? Down the shaft?"

She knew me. "Do I have a choice, madame?"

Not if I valued bed, board and an occasional gust of human conversation. She explained that, beyond the cavernous dormitories of the Pit, there were in AUNTY's domain all the former 10¢ four-by-four urinals from here to West Poolesville, with the toilets removed, among other ingenious discouragements.

I chose the Pit. AUNTY Quartermistress Clinkscale showed me down. Otherwise like her sisters, Clinkscale had a faint blush under her calloused cheeks and her floral coiffure was always engagingly disheveled. After Ames and Anvil, she was the junior member of AUNTY. The three of them carried the standard, in the absence of apelike attendants, against defenestration, overeager defecation, round-the-clock public masturbation, and other common vices of the insane.

By 10 a.m. I had learned that in the Pit life was divided, or rather axed, into two halves, *presents* and *duties*.

First, presents. Life was a present. Sleep, tins of lard-fried potatoes and bacon ends, a body preserved from leprosy if not a flea or two, winter afternoons in the company of one's peers, all milling and muttering around the dayroom in laundered hospital togas...all these were presents. As if this weren't enough, I learned that Yeeza and Clinkscale had appointed themselves Yule and Birthday stewardesses respectively.

At 10:30 a.m., we were gently flagellated into motion over a long deal table spread with popsicle sticks, glue, pot holder sets, macaroni, ligatoni, sequins, glass beads, twine, crayons, vegetable coloring. These we transformed into blanket-stitch antimacassars, wire clotheshangers wound with yarn, little soaps in the shape of malignant lymph nodes, blind pulls, etc.

While every day was Birthday, Yule, relative to prosperity and overcrowding, came whenever the Yule box was full. A Yule meter on the top informed the interested on the progress of the approaching holiday: I noticed when I came it stood a third short of New Year's.

At noon AUNTY ran the receiving kitchen, out of sheer arrant despotism, with necrophiliac overtones, since it had better run itself, with the pots tightly closed and the diners gagged and blindfolded. Instead the ladies fussed over the steam trays, peering with deep and unseemly fascination into the soup pots the dumbwaiter brought down, imposing home-spun titles like *Mobile porkpie* on esoteric stewballs that floated in grayish seas of sauce...

Now for duties, since, as one suspected, no present without its duty. Life was in fact a duty. In accordance with this philosophy, the Depot laundry chutes, converging from all eight upper levels, debouched with regular woofs at the far end of the dayroom.

At 1:00 p.m. AUNTY directed a drill, since lasting was a part of duty. For calisthenics each AUNTY wore a stainless steel cop whistle on a gimp lanyard filched from the Yule box, as well as blue gymnasium bloomers that revealed, in all three, another common trait: they all had kneecaps so fitly clapped onto the joint as to seem to hump out at the back.

At 1:30, AUNTY ran the laundry, from a little slatted and glassed-in cubicle with a great horizontal fan hanging under fluorescent tubes. From here they directed the patients with megaphones that could be heard from time to time over the gag and regorge of the washers. They called breaks, doled out smokes every thirty minutes, and sent up shifts to the lavatories.

At 2:00 I took a look at myself, folding jockey shorts for size 34 lectors after spending the morning milling confetti from obsolete Depot correspondence. The conclusion was simple.

"This can't go on for two weeks." And I sat down on a pile of sheets to consider the situation.

In seconds Clinkscale came trotting out of the cubicle. "Let's go, get moving, no ciggies for slackers, or it's toilet detail in the morning." Nevertheless I was encouraged by a broad smile and a scalloped flush up her cheekbones...

"I'm bushed," I said. "How about if we give each other backrubs in the linen closet?"

"Of all the crust!" But her bosom swelled up against my shoulder. "I wouldn't believe all the stuff I read in the broadsides if I were you, Hughby..."

Of course I began to think of the broadsides and to prickle behind the ears.

> As for the other AUNTY dames
> We know them all when we know AMES
>
> She takes temptation up the c***...
>
> To hell with food, she'd rather f***...

Annie's satire on her skinny rivals was off the mark for Clinkscale, I thought. She surely was in no danger of starving to death. To prove it she pressed her big thigh against my lap, hard.

"No, no," I agreed vaguely, "not all the stuff..." She turned and I followed her large low buns to the linen closet.

Life was a present. She made me lie down on the stacked bales of facetowels. I was not to kiss her. She pulled my hospital toga up with a jerk and gathered my prick into the warm rabbithole of her cheeks. I came in, O, ten seconds. "Magnificent! Thank you." She patted my forehead. I confessed my inexperience. She chuckled.

She began running her tongue up and down my abdomen. She had a flat porous tongue with the lie of a feather. "Stay still." And she draped a facecloth over my eyes.

"Don't go!"

93

"I'm just working up the next couplet, gentle broadside reader."

I sighed happily. "Do you think I could stay in the nuthouse till spring, Clinkscale?"

The tap hissed on and off. "A friend of sister Analarge's? Your credit's always good."

It was this remark, though sweetly uttered, that saved my cock from destruction. Suddenly uneasy, I peeked around the terrycloth. A green glass bottle stood open by a basin. It was the laundry lye. At the same instant I caught sight of two pairs of eyes staring through niches in the shelving.

Then I ran! I swept all the beads from the tables to trip the girls up. AUNTY pursued me, but I was safe on the second level landing before they piled into the stairwell.

"Annie-lover!"

"Piggy dog of a cornholing cuntsucker!"

"Abortion ears!"

That was my last sight of AUNTY underground, shaking her fists, spitting up at me, chattering through her teeth.

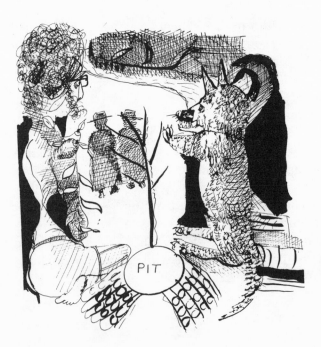

XIV
Diagnosis

I was out of the bughouse, but school had lost its savor.

I developed chest pains, and stayed in my phone booth in the subway two weeks. Happy interlude! When these symptoms gave way, I burst into tears. I was consoled for my attachment by an evening of one-line gags for the intestines. Then perhaps I asked too much, triple quartan Sump malaria with dysentery...

In the morning I crept into the doctor's laboratory block by a door in the pantry, and stole an old stethoscope. I felt perfectly well. But surely I had cause to hope! Back in my phone booth, I got the thing into position. Now to prop up my sagging self-possession with the giant wedge of a guarded prognosis. I wasn't choosy, I would have settled for anything, Sousa to Basin Street, as long as it wasn't the same old two-step, coil and recoil.

Instead I heard nothing, nothing at all.

In my distress I ran, why deny it, directly to Analarge. Now this was a Saturday, hours after the sham topos would have gone on show, had the masters not thought I was safe in the asylum. Whatever the hour, it was deep in the doctor's day off. The gargoyled padlock hung on the vestibule door.

I slipped in through the pantry. The doctor reclined in his facial-surgical chair, receiving a shave at the capable hands of

Empory Harfanger, who also turned pages of the doctor's notebooks (open on the footrest) subsequent to his grunts, which were rather many than varied. Doctor Analarge read, at a staggering speed, upside down and backwards via the overhead mirror.

I closed the pantry door behind me. "Examine me!"

I had never before this time been sick before the doctor.

Analarge bared his teeth. I could see this in the overhead mirror, where he hung out amid banks of foam like a moray eel from its hole in the sea sludge.

I pressed my case. "My heart beat has blown! I can't hear a thing. In this state I can't truckle to the 'Nope' of constabulary out-to-lunchism. At a time like this you won't twit your ordinance in my face…"

"*Fech!*" roared the doctor at length. Cushions of lather sailed through the air, suffusing the lab with the powerful scent of camellias. Now he spoke, not to me but to Empory: "It's Saturday night, by god. May I burst if I hang up my sole recreation for any man's ails but my own. Be he doubled over! Be his eye ridges stuck to his cold great toes by the stale scum of a bedsore. I don't care! Let him croak. I am not on call, I am soloing, soloing, intractably soloing. This communal leech bit moves me not at all. Shave on."

Empory shaved in silence, hooking the doctor's nostril on his forefinger and lifting it clear of the passing blade.

I persevered, through fasting and meditation. Soon I took heart. The doctor's grunts to his page-turner slowed and died away, though he kept his eye on the mirror. In the end he fanned out his fingers in front of his jowls, and Empory stepped away.

The doctor pointed at me. "Empory, what do we do for a mild to acute case of acid indiscretion, of no experimental kick whatsoever?"

Empory strained to recall. He laid the razor aside on the footrest, pulled his chin, tapped his foot, and finally stole a glance at the doctor, who was absently admiring his homemade teeth in the overhead mirror. Empory wised up then and, scratching his head, said, "Why, that syndrome, doctor, escapes me utterly."

"Hmmm," said Analarge. "Well, let us expand your diagnostic proclivities. Look over this wretch to my rear! But I'll tell you right off, son, it's asking too much at my age and stage to play doctor." He got to his feet. "So take your time, and if you need me, drop the whole thing. I'm out." And he slipped his notebooks down the seat of his Turkish bloomers and went up the ladder to the laboratory loft, sniffing loudly en route over the residue of camellia froth on his upper lip.

At 5:00 in the morning the doctor came sliding back down the pole in his crumpled pyjamas, trailing the black thunderhead of a Perfecto #1. Empory sat across from me rapt in a crossword puzzle, while I sat snivelling into the hospital gown he had grudgingly reissued me for the purpose—to keep me quiet after he terminated my examination.

As my silence was under orders from Empory, likewise his orders were under orders from Analarge, *viz.*, to keep my unsound person out of his overtaxed eyeshot and earshot. But Empory had honored these instructions not from awe but from strategy, the better to corner the doctor when he came down later on, as he had just done, as he always did, to water his peaplants and putter around in sweet and unresponsible solitude at the break of day.

What a mistake! Doctor Analarge did a little cowering jig, first in shock, then in gross primitive disappointment. "And the hell of it, Harfanger, is why if you were going to extract my edict on this, this immaculate deception by hook or crook, why you didn't put the squeeze on me six and a half hours ago, instead of hanging around to worm into my nighty, my garden and my peace of mind?"

"But I did look him over," said Empory blandly. "There's nothing wrong with him at all."

"No, no," said the doctor.

"—that I can tell," said Empory. Too late, he was finished!

"Do tell!" said Analarge. "Well put! Well, go on with it, test-tube head! Your timely replacement is beating down my door, begging for orders. Do I need you? I need you like fun!"

He backed Empory towards the vestibule. As he passed me I reached out and stuck the stethoscope in his face. "That thing!" He took it, shook it, and pitched it in the garbage.

"He's got those ear bobs..." said the assistant, stumbling out into the dawn.

"Ear bobs! Listen here!—

HIM?
He's got what he deserves!
A low muttering case of cornute* *acarpia***
What he wants is my little Annie-bag in his bed
to get up his bodily heat

Well forget it!
Look Shamp!
Why should anybody take so much grief?
You ain't nothing but a living burgeoning self-suffering
plasma-looting tropos of secondary sexual character,
a piss-ear, a PERSONALITY !
NOW QUIT MY SIGHT!"

This text, with two carbons, lay on the escritoire in the vestibule.

I left without a word—well, one word.

I confess the ending to this episode hangs from a small corruption in the text, which I doctored myself, with a nickel eraser.

Please to substitute *acardia**** for *acarpia*, and you will catch my meaning, one tragic—mortal—in extent.

No heart! No heart!

A discouraging diagnosis. But as I walked from the lab to the subway along the Sumpsky Prospect, the crossfire of sun

---

*horny
**fruitlessness
***no heart!

shooting out of the aspens struck me square across the ear bobs, and in that light I reconsidered the matter.

Sump malaria was bad. But no heart! Surely this was an extraordinary diagnosis.

This was not to say Analarge bore me a grudge, or had deliberately sunk this huge and terminal vacuole into my expectations. But how had he used me to date—as the sham topos, for instance—except as a freak? Because I had ear wattles. And what were a pair of ear wattles flapping in the breeze beside this perfect monstrosity of omission? No heart! Well, not so fast. What was the doctor's unnatural lust for the last thing in bodily curiosities? Surely this new, so-called "heartlessness" of mine was only in tune with his excess of zeal!

I stuck a change of socks in my lector's jacket pocket and began jogging down the tubes toward the city-solo. I would go to Bertolt Borigard, a Big Yolk Cup goalie twenty years since, now an amateur lector best known for his soft-shoe riff interspersed with paternal asides, a zero to Shipoff's taste, who pursued a little medicine to boot. His nameplate gleamed just over the Arsleverings' footbridge, a few feet from the tube ramp on the Big Yolk bank.

The white-haired ex-hockey ace received me in an ill-concealed welter of *weltpolitik* and pride. Suddenly abashed, I realized that to Borigard the Depot was the temple of his worldly competition. There I was in his eyeball, an early refugee of the Shipovian subway, a human mineshaft of information, timely topos, power.

I sank into a chair. What had I done? "Beebee" Borigard stood before me, quaking with joy. If news of this sidetrip slipped over the river to the Depot, my career as a Topical Tropist was over.

To lose it all! All at once I felt framed and hounded, exploited in the ear wattles, neglected in the mastery of the voice, wounded in the tropos I'd turned over to the masters until now, age 17, I'd almost thrown it all away.

"What are these?" said Borigard, fingering my ear wattles.

"Never mind!" I smacked away his hand.

"Well, son?"

"Well what?"

"What's the problem?"

"No heart."

"No heart!" he said, winking like a nocturnal tarsier. "That could be serious. Let's have a look." He opened the hospital gown to my waist, and went very slowly, chuckling and tapping with his big dry fingers. In the end he peered benignly down at my hairless breastbone:

"I'll put it this way, young fellow. What has a few outlets, a few chambers, is in charge of the works, eh, and beats, beats like crazy?" He pinched my cheek.

I stared. Behind him, through layers of grayish windowpane the great city appeared, steep and rigid. The description was exact. It was the exemplary topos of heartlessness! The House-Father.

I invoked St. Cornwallis for the hazards of power. But I had no power! A House-Father! Here was a fatality I hadn't even taken into consideration.

I took off for the office door. I must have gone out by way of the pane, for when he was ready, old Borigard sent me an enormous bill.

As I charged down the sidewalk towards the Great Morass at the city center, I had one last sight of the paternal wise-cracker leaning up to his nuts out of the sixteenth floor window.

"Shamp! But naturally you have a heart! Did you ever doubt it? Everybody has a heart!"

O yeah? And when was I born, Beeb? The end of last week?

XV

Tapsvine

I ran until the deepening bog let go of each leg only reluctantly, teasingly, after a long pull—even so I ran against the suck till I went down. There I lay, twitching on a bun of marsh grass, cool, rank, and bulging to east where far above and beyond me the Arslevering big top twinkled on its tuft, seeming to my dizziness to wheel over and over, even down toward the bog where I lay.

It was May eve, a night of the quality of gnats' wings, the air full of restless motion, not unkind.

One point had to be revised without delay: I had a heart, I could feel it, jumping up and down on my lifeless crasis like a thing with a life all its own.

All its own, that was it. So it came and went like the rest of my topos, feckless host to itinerant particles that I was. And what was I but their penny ante deal in the barroom of the Central Hotel, in some jerkwater town, once left, unrediscoverable? What was I but an oath shouted into the windstream in the Ozarks, between two demented Greyhound busdrivers, passing east to Sedalia, and west to Des Moines? Or was it I that went, no more than a stumbling track between a pay toilet and a coin telephone, a stranger dropping off mnemosynic macromolecules, like dimes through sewer grilles, to the memories of strange masters, from Brakeknot even to Borigard?

And this was the Shamp who heard he was a House-Father and believed it—of the Depot, no less. O no—he-he-ha-ha-ho-ho-ho-haw, O no! For here I was, myself, Shamp, laid out in a salt bog, a compound complex compost heap so unstable and far-fetched I could barely qualify for charlady, much less master, of myself, never mind the Depot. Or how could I mop and pastewax that of which I was stumped to say what it was, or even lay you two dollars that it was?

"One is a crowd," the doctor had said—he could toss that off. The epigram rose heavily over my head, like a park pigeon. He knew! Small wonder his life was a blind sauté from one frying pan to another.

I thought back to my meeting with Shipoff, his discovery of me under the horse chestnut, his starry seduction-geschnort, 2-penny-a-line, and the sincere puerility with which I threw in my lot with his, all for a mistake. His mistake—that he took my wellworn topos during Brakeknot's ceasefire as noncontingent, gratuitous, the spontaneous rage of a great soul in solitude. Then out went Brakeknot, bosom enemy, lover of the art. In came my invitation—to a rabid foxtrot, my name in waxy dress pumps, a floorful of six-toed decals to dog between lessons from the master in person, there in the heart of the West Poolesville dump, a mere two-mile whiff from the city-solo—all mine provided I took it with a smile in the asshole, and failing that, or even, by Chrust! providing it, provided I also trimmed the bugger's nails as called for, hooked his truss cinches, fried his Chinese onion rings, ran his britches to the presser, took up his boyfriend's consort's time, and peed on his enemies, or even his friends upon occasion.

Well! Surely that flight toward the city-solo with Shipoff had only made muck of the hope that inspired it. And yet the abortion of that hope still bawled on the table, pinguid and shiny with the lube of delivery. If I was a prophet at all, it was Brakeknot who had anointed me—and coot spittle though it was, in vain I now foraged the Big Yolk skyline, from my back, for one mirroring droplet as fit for my topos by half as the merest particle, the millionth part, of Brakeknot's smallest sneeze, always sneezed in my honor, were it only to wish me influenza and an early grave.

"Brakeknot!" I cried out, "Brakeknot! respects and diuturnity from the member in Big Yolk!"

(May some misfit of the world I leave behind dignify my retirement with like expostulations.)

"Brakeknot! Come out! A bilateral ceasefire on the year's softest midnight. What say to a rubber of honeymoon bridge between trenches? What distance too much for you, immortal traveller? What can Bulimy hold for the likes of Brakeknot, when Big Yolk holds the likes of me, by the styrofoam balls in a salt bog no less."

I heaved a sigh.

A match struck in the darkness.

"Quake, brother, and the bog quakes with you. Not a point in its favor! Have the goodness to sit up and compose yourself."

Behind the pink coal of smoke, a face appeared, long and hollow, with gray Cathay mustaches dangling on either side of a gold-tipped cigarette. I saw two small starry eyes set in puffballs of gray lashes, eyes which, once spotted in the light, went on shining in the darkness that followed.

"As for honeymoon bridge, save it for your honeymoon. How about gin, say a nickel a point, double for skunk?" A deck of cards clacked down. "Cut!" He poked in a pail with a stick. Little flames came and went along the top of it, gold wavelets over an invisible mesa. The stick took fire; he lit a hurricane lamp. "A little illumination!"

He sat among ragged furs, cigarette papers, lard cans, fire-blackened crockery. His back was propped on the crumbly riser of a footbridge. A fine leather valise gleamed to his rear, the halflight licking the emblem, GULF LINKS C.C. A club out of reach of even Doctor Analarge's connections! Its owner's feet all the same were wrapped in three yards of towel pinched from some restroom dispenser, full of handprints. They rested on a fat coil of combat firehose in camouflage colors. Against the tepid draft he wore a monk's cowl, hitched together with a tin election button:

"Three cents a point?"

I stared at him.

"On the cuff? A pox! Gentleman's gin!" He shrugged and lay back.

The smoke of his cigarette curled up the bridge piers and hung below the pavement in loops which faded as they flattened. Just so had my hopes, I thought, percolated from the Depot towards the stratosphere, only to flatten on the smog ceiling, neck and neck with the dryer exhaust and the fumes from the shitcan...

He stuck his cigarette into the mud. "What brings you to the bog, little brother? What did you do, kick in a shoe store?" And he cast an interested eye on my dress pumps. Suddenly I struck myself in the forehead. The black patent leather stuck out of a hospital gown—I had left my lector's duds in Beebee Borigard's office.

"Well, that sews it up, Shamp: back to the minors."

"What do you take me for, a stool pigeon?" he said. "What do I care what you kick in? My record couldn't use yours for a footnote." He laughed. "What do you think brings me to the Great Morass—a surfeit of popular acclaim perhaps!"

"I have my enemies," I said.

"My enemies, little brother, have a heading in the Yellow Pages. Two, for the rival factions. Such is the love of Providence for soreheads in unwieldy clumps—they undergo mitosis. In the natural history of slobbering monomania, I'm a martyr ... Smoke? Now who's on your tail?"

"I did it to myself!"

"Ah, noble sentiments. And who's this Grapeshot? Breaksod? Your rap partner? The one that got sent up."

He leaned closer to inspect me. "Caramba! what's with the ear lobes? Is it catching? Pox! Whew! Weird!"

"You don't like them?"

"Ah-hah! You're a fugitive from quarantine."

It was good to be sure. I grabbed, and began yanking my ear bobs with all the strength I had left.

"Hold on there—you'll hurt yourself—let off—"

"My future—star sham of the Depot—Thanksgiving with all the little SHIPOFFS!" I pulled harder.

"The Depot...one of Shipoff's boys, eh? You're the star sham?"

"Prime draw, the Grand Tour!"

"Let off them, they're swelling like paw paws." He pulled my hands down. "Listen close, here's a deal for you. If I put a little living room between you and those doo-dads, will you do me a service?"

"Anything!"

"Okay!"—and he pointed a long finger at me. "Go back and tell your boss he should give me a plug when he boosts my ideas. O, well I remember. That was Little Athens in nineteen-and-what...? A murderous shindig if I ever saw one. Now he's milking that Ox Roast when I barely missed lynching. Does he think I'm dead? Senile? Or possibly kindhearted?"

"The World-Friar Tapsvine!"

He smiled. "Shall I autograph your ear flaps on the way out?"

But it was not his autograph I wanted. For it took only the crudest instant S.C.O.R. to figure the impact it would have on past masters if I showed at the Depot with the World-Friar in tow. On the arm of a master of the World-Friar's proportions! They would recoil...

My topos was resurrected.

"Forceps...clamps...shears...cauteries..." He fished through his valise. "All set? Don't forget now! he should give me a plug or regret it—I'll catch up with him soon enough. And you too if you turn me around, little brother."

"Don't worry!" I said. "Just do it. Take them off."

He chuckled, holding a silk handkerchief at the corners. "Now you see it, now you don't." And he tied it around my eyes. A rasp made short strokes over metal and clinked down. He was humming.

"O I well remember all right. I took a shit and the turds came flying out after me." There were two quick snips. "And the Arslevering pueblo sank another yard. It ought to be condemned, that overdecorated quonset hut." Two hisses and the handkerchief flew off. My late ear wattles lay in my lap quite bloodless, like windfalls in an orchard yard.

"All over. And cured in formaldehyde..." He dropped them in a ball jar.

"You can keep them, doc!"

"I will, don't worry. Odd pieces. Never seen anything quite like them. They'll fit right in between a Mundurucu mother mollifier and the sworn and testified buboes of St. Roche, stuffed with goosedown. Just think, little brother—if you flop as a lector, your immortality is assured all the same, just on the strength of your ear growths in the World-Friar's museum. What was that name?"

"Hughbury Shamp."

He wrote it on the label. "A fortunate encounter all around, my dear fellow"—he extended his hand—"so take off! and keep your word."

But I only handed him back his silk handkerchief.

"Well? Are you feeling separation pangs along the ear lobes?" He turned back to his valise and pulled out a hypodermic. "Little brother, you should enjoy a little sting like that. It's a crime to throw the astrodisiac away on corporeal afflictions."

"Brother Tapsvine, I can't go back to the Depot—"

He turned sharply, and his eyes made my forehead prickle.

"—without you."

"I see." The needle rolled away across the blanket. Slowly he reached for yet another cigarette, then leaned back thoughtfully against the riser. I rushed with his match. After a while he said, "Pusillanimous the means! O chicken! But no one pigeons Tapsvine lightly...I see your intention, though yellow-bellied, was survival. I can go along with that! You're entitled to that position, so long as you don't make a public nuisance of yourself.

"Personally, I oppose population..."

"That's Shipoff's star topos, the over-population bomb," I yawned.

"Who said anything about *over*-population?"

Tapsvine began folding and filling his valise. "Tell me, who runs religion at the Depot these days? That Analarge fellow? What's his line?"

"Formerly cosmetic surgery and galenicals...now almost nothing but the hard core Inexpressible..."

"Scratch that burnout. Who else counts, besides Shipoff?"

"That's it."

"No religion! Glad to hear it. I'm inflamed with missionary zeal. Where's my mustache comb—pox, a lost cause in this light. I'll miss Nana, but she can take care of herself. Do you like snakes, little brother?"

"No, sir!"

"You haven't met the right ones."

"Uncle Shipoff..."

He raised a finger at me. "Indiscreet! You can get along with snakes. They're one-track minded, but utterly dependable in their simplicity. They like their comfort." He bent over and patted that coil, that combat firehose, by his ankles. "They are dumb! Likewise the human variety...

"*Hasta la vista*, Nana—soon!" He poured the last third of a bottle of crème de cacao into a saucer. "My anaconda," he said, rubbing his bare toe over her back. "Self-supporting, mine only in the bias of her heart, if she has one." The World-Friar picked up his valise. "Go in health, Nana, but stay off the hill, stay away from Little Athens. If you value your gizzard, abstain from Arsleverings. They require long curing."

XVI
Great Aunt Maiseen

I trotted up the Sumpsky Prospect in the World-Friar's Verdun greatcoat, so long it swept the petals off the buttercups. Suddenly a round of buckshot peppered the aspen tops over my head. A few steps behind me, Tapsvine gave a low whistle. Little twigs rained down on our shoulders, then tiny green banderoles, once leaves.

"Get back, Hughby! I don't know where you left those ear bobs off but you do!"

"Shipoff, meet—"

"O no Hughby. After striking out on your own in the city-solo you don't just pop home to the Depot bare-eared. You're up to your ears in shit!"

But even as he shouted, Tapsvine strolled out into shooting range, his World-Friar underpinnings lit up in the balmy moonlight. Shipoff hardly required the insignia. Hadn't he studied Tapsvine's portrait on the overleaf of each slim volume he filched from the Mohorovocic Library, by the glow of his kerosene stove on nights too cold to sleep?

True, hanged if I could have recognized Tapsvine from the World-Friar gaucho of the frontispiece, all *cintas*, *bigotes*, and silver plate. Shipoff, however, knew him at once.

He came running up the upramp, his little hand stuck out in front of him. "Welcome! You've gone gray, Tapsvine. But it suits you, the hair-raising charm of your narrow escapes—"

Tapsvine bowed. "Kind of you to notice, Shipoff. The fact is the escapes that bristled me were not mine but my enemies'— for every passé homicidal impulse, a silver blade of hair. Such well-polled civilization taxes the durability…"

Arm in arm they rambled down the upramp towards the Grand Concourse.

My ear wattles temporarily forgotten, I started for the lector's clothes bin, but at the last moment Tapsvine held my sleeve. He liked me in the beginning. Nor had I taken the time, it's true, to confess my trials to the World-Friar end to end. And yet I believe that the urbane Tapsvine would have pardoned all of it, the blabbering, the poltroonery, the hypochondria, everything, and kept me on as his toady to this day, if Shipoff hadn't hauled my crimes to court one day pre Ox Roast. That showdown was too priceless, too bizarre for the World-Friar to pass up.

But now he held my sleeve. We shook hands. "Hughbury, I'm grateful. You have set my feet in a large room. And think of this room with two pool tables, a friendly bookmaker, a flurry of barmaids of lamentable morality…"

He sat down on Shipoff's bench and patted the cushion beside him. "We'll share, brother Shipoff. I know whose room this is! Depend on the World-Friar Tapsvine to worm the Depot floor plan out of the punk on the long walk over. He's a good boy, Shipoff, unusual. Freehearted. And the *radix malorum* of the age is greed, agreed? Overcrowding is only a mechanical dysfunction, overadaptation unto slobbery in man." He patted Shipoff's thigh in its houndstooth trousers. "Clean up your act! Yield to your generous impulses. Make room for an old Aswan crocodile fancier like yourself. In fact, make room for an old crocodile like yourself!" And he suddenly snapped his jaws under Shipoff's nose.

Jerking backwards, the lectromagnate's head thumped off the wall tiles. I smiled, a mistake—seeing me behind Tapsvine, Shipoff went to the trouble of prophetically ripping me into small particles between his thumb and forefingers. "It's still my Depot, boys. I have the deed and I can dump you both."

Tapsvine shrugged. "Knock yourself out. Everything that belongs to the body streams like the Sump. If you're going to take my Hibernation topos to the lectern, I'm going to revive religion at your Depot, and we'll split the take fifty-fifty. I want my piece, Shipoff."

"Piece of what? These are hard times, Tapsvine."

"Would you lie to the World-Friar, Brother Shipoff?"

"Zealously! I would lie to my sainted mother, if it helped me. But even the treacherous vermin"—(he pointed at me)—"will confirm that when he fled the Depot last week for greener lecterns, this was my whole savings." He reached in his pocket and pulled out a mutilated quarter. "Of course this is no ordinary two-bits. Observe these longwise gashes. The six-wheeler that did in this coin sliced our late favorite son Senator Arslevering in two at the same time, when he leaned too far out of the subway window for a prairie butterfly, barnstorming through West Hinnstead...

"Nevertheless this historic quarter is yours for any flat coin of the same denomination, of even the crassest inexperience..."

Tapsvine turned to me. "What's the story?"

"Well," I smiled feebly, "it's true it won't work in the Depot washing machine." For Shipoff told the truth—times were even harder than before the days of the Sham. The lectromagnate's collar was pearly with hair oil, indicating that McCorkle had not come across with the household money for weeks. And what hair oil! The bear cave odor of petrolated laurel leaves could seep off nothing but Alto Grizzard's English Formula, as often as Shipoff had sworn that before he'd touch that stuff, he'd starve.

"I am starved," he explained.

The World-Friar stood up in disgust. "A pox, you should be doing better than this, brother Shipoff. Your name is all over the city-solo. How can you have a name in Big Yolk and no cash? Are you playing the horses? What's your boyfriend

McCorkle doing up there at the Arslevering pueblo, incinerating his allowance?"

"How do you mean, my boyfriend McCorkle?" Shipoff said sullenly.

"I know everything that goes on up on the hill. Listen, Shipoff, I reeled in more backers at those weekly freakshows in their heyday than you'll ever pry off the hook, and not for half such worthy causes. I don't understand…"

Shipoff threw up his hands. "Okay! That Texarkana closet queen McCorkle, what a zero. He hasn't got the presence to keep the floor and ceiling from flying at each other."

"But he's a beauty queen, that one."

"Never mind what he looks like, when he walks into a room, the rafters creak from the nosedive in atmospheric pressure. My ears even pop…"

"He can't move Vasselina?"

"Not anymore. And I can't find anybody she likes enough to move him out."

Their voices dropped. Tapsvine jotted some figures, and Shipoff began to whisper in his succulent way, the steam of his syllables curling softly up Tapsvine's right ear, across his gray crewcut, and down the left. The two looked over at me now and then, snickering at the World-Friar's greatcoat leaning against the wall with my wrists and ankles sticking out of it. What else was funny?

"Airy bones…"

"Late fire engine ear bobs…"

"Somebuddy Greatsnot…"

They snorted from time to time between sibilants.

On my feet, I drifted. Spring moved under the World-Friar's greatcoat. I felt, well, a small insect between the lapels and peeked in at my chest. A hair had appeared there. It gleamed in the moonlight sticking out roughly straight from between my nipples like a barge pole. Looking up, I saw the moon raft slowly across the round blue hole that was the subway exit. I stood there feeling drowned and restless, the cool beam waxing my cheeks like rice paddies. For once the idea of my face as a surface engaging or not was lost to me: instead it felt good to be blind and unborn, to close my lids against the moonlight, incubating under them the scalded red eye of a possum. Only stupefaction seemed equal to the spring, which pried at all my sense holes as cruelly as a virgin.

The voices went on behind me:

"Ersatz island sub-species…"

Suddenly I hoped for someone to come by the exit and look at me. I wanted to gleam in his eye like an ingot, like pig iron.

There were footsteps immediately.

Soon Alto Grizzard came scratching down the Sumpsky Prospect on his cautious toeballs, for his regular evening prowl. He looked at me. Then he looked again, put on his glasses and squinted over them. Just as his eyes went round, he spotted the World-Friar and Shipoff murmuring on the bench. His neck craned around the upramp. I rooted myself in his eyeshot, dead center. He waved frantically for me to move, mouthing soundless syllables and jerking his finger up and down.

The WWWoooORRrrLLLLD—FfRIIIaaaar??? Heeeeeeeeere?

Was it possible? Alto Grizzard, jowls, chins and fingers all twitching in exasperation, was pumping me for info! I was being interrogated in sign language by the same Alto Grizzard who snatched his satchel of hair oil samples into the toilet booth with him as soon as I staggered into the lavatory in the a.m., and even opened the door a faint crack with his toe as he groaned on the bowl, to keep an eye on me shaving three sinks up from his dimestore towel.

Suddenly it seemed good to me to shake my fist at him. The World-Friar's coat fell open, and I caught the glassy flicker of my new hair snapping out. Grizzard gasped at my nakedness, and hurried away.

Behind me glasses clinked. With their elbows linked, Shipoff and the World-Friar Tapsvine were having a schnapps and seltzer, looking appreciatively not at each other but at me.

Shipoff began: "Hughby, if a man have a candle up his snort, shall he hide it under—"

Tapsvine waved him aside. "No, let's speak of the crust. In signing yourself over for an education, little brother, never fume about the crust, the vessel that surrounds you, the dead skin—"

"My skin! Not a chance. What do you want with my skin?" I said warily.

"You're young, it's spring."

"I'm here to orate my topos from a lectern in the city-solo. In my skin!"

"What's all this?" Tapsvine said.

Shipoff shrugged. "Some kind of sentimental attachment to his skin."

"A vice," Tapsvine cried. "Skin has nothing to do with a lectern in Big Yolk. Skin, Shipoff. Didn't that go out with furbelows and celluloid shirt-fronts?"

"If it's Vasselina Arslevering you're skinning me for, you can forget it," I said.

"Forget it..." Tapsvine repeated. He scratched the little cleft between his mustaches. "Arslevering...what did we forget... the Ox Roast, Shipoff! The Arslevering Midsummer's Day Ox Roast, my man." He sighed with relief. "There's the payroll, if we can just hold out two more months without stretching the point."

"Stretching it!" Shipoff lay back with the seltzer bottle behind his neck. "When the Ox Roast comes near, I try to shrink my point to the verge of invisibility, and right over the edge if possible. Are you going? You can stretch it."

"You turned it down?" Tapsvine said in disbelief. "You're letting the Tropists sit out the Ox Roast and Colloquium on Polity? You're a dead man." He started for the upramp.

Shipoff opened one eye. "I'm a live man. What's more I'm a smart man. For that reason I steer by the Arslevering Midsummer Wild West powder spree. I even begged my way into the keynote slot at the Bosky Point Lighthouse Bonfire, just to get as far on the other side of the Sump as possible."

"He has a sentimental regard for his intact neck and cranium," I said, "notwithstanding all that went out with pig-pulling."

"Unbelievable," Tapsvine said at the exit. "Go to Bosky Point when the Ox Roast is running! Unpardonable. When you have my topos! When you owe me money!"

With his bench all to himself, Shipoff rolled over on his belly. "You've been out of the country, Tapsvine. Did you know that last year the Arsleverings set up a thirty-bed first-aid station in the lawn furniture storeroom? Did you know that thirty speakers ended up on those chaise-longues, and every one of them had his name, address and choice of embalming fluid tied to his big toe by lunchtime?"

"Pox!" Tapsvine said, still standing in the upramp, "what's a little firebomb epidemic when two million dollars in grant money hangs in the balance? Besides this year Little Athens will be crawling with plainclothes cops, ergo my reluctance for staging a comeback..."

Shipoff droned on: *"De rigueur* for every terrorist east of the Blue Ridge. The Independent Schizo's Non-Invitational Annual Open: 3.75 stiffs per hour, a twenty percent mortality rate for the opening day speakers alone..."

The World-Friar came back to the bench, ignoring this catalog. "Besides, brother Shipoff, I confess I lack the proper ambition. It's true I love fame. Dissolute? yes I am. Bossy? I am. Plundering. I am. Socially inimical? gee-haw, check—but ambition?—I spit on it." And he spat, pa-*chiiing*, into the crown of Shipoff's golfing cap, which rang out like a cash register. The World-Friar had lost his patience, and in order to talk into Shipoff's face he leaned on the back of the bench and rolled the lectromagnate over. But his other hand plunged through the rotten upholstery and he fell onto Shipoff, springs up to his armpit.

115

Stuck so the two masters stared at each other, nose against nose.

"I believe I see your point at last," Shipoff said, "since it's sticking me right between the eyebrows. But who is the rational choice between the two of us for the Ox Roast after all? You're the real pop of the Hibernation topos, you're the World-Friar, they've been waiting for you. If we really want to make a killing let's have Tapsvine home in on Little Athens after five ymfffff—"

Tapsvine's elbow shifted into Shipoff's mouth. "After five years?" he said. "Where do you think I've been for five years? Where would a man of my interests be on Midsummer's Day but the Arslevering Ox Roast—last year for example?" And all at once an athletic spinster bawled out of the World-Friar's voicebox:

"Dishy! Da buss your Great-Aunty Maiseen!"

"Mffffff," cried Shipoff, with troubled eyes. That is, *Dishy!* For he recognized that rarely used nickname of Vasselina's, a family name wholly unfamiliar to the public.

Worse yet, he recognized that line! The greeting that Tapsvine had just uttered was the same that Vasselina's Great-Aunt Maiseen Billow spoke through her tears when she turned up on the eve of last year's Ox Roast, wearing striped cotton stockings and flannel overskirts in fashion thirty years before, when she had been the best known horsewoman in New Zealand. Her enormous sea trunk was hauled up the Arslevering tuft by tractor trailer and unloaded in back of the summer pavilion, being far too large to fit through the portico. She seemed to have packed for a long stay.

It was an emotional reunion. Maiseen presided at the Midsummer's Eve supper table, amid bounteous toasts. Later, drunk, and despondent over the number of Arslevering relations who had departed forever from the family table, she stumbled pathetically about the summerhouse until she could be covered with a featherbed, on Vasselina's tender instruc-

116

tions, wherever she happened to pass out: as it was, on the floor of her late brother Hardy's library.

The next afternoon, in the thick of the firebombing, the supposed Great-Aunt Maiseen Billow disappeared forever down Tenth Avenue toward the Big Yolk docks, breezing a huge chestnut quarterhorse that two Delta gambler-breeders among the guests later swore under oath to have been Soltero, the famed Natchez stud. It was then discovered that all of the cash for flat grant endowments had been cleaned out of brother Hardy's library safe—some $90,000.

Months later the actual Maiseen Billow was located in a wretched salt pork-and-potato nursing home on a farm near Gisborne, where, only marginally oriented and without known family, she had been ruthlessly milked by the proprietor couple since a dimly remembered riding accident eleven years before.

The imposter Great-Aunt Maiseen's immense trunk behind the summerhouse was forced open. It was simply a stall, littered with horse manure and drained vials of injectable cocaine...

Hence Shipoff's eyes, troubled like the Sump in April.

"So I've done my Ox Roast bit," Tapsvine finished. "As for your Depot, I'm here strictly to advise, to modernize your religious interiors, but most of all—to get my divvies." Carefully he raised his elbow from Shipoff's mouth.

But the lectromagnate, far from shouting protests, only gazed past him at some bubble floating near the ceiling, his eyes slowly mulling back to their old sour gravy color, or something even sourer, Aucklander sheep dung, or puce.

Tapsvine squinted down at him. "Of course, the fact that I'm not going to stick my neck out at this year's Ox Roast is no special reason why you should stick out yours. Use a proxy!"

Shipoff nodded insensibly. I tell you, he was defeated! Never before and not for long, but just now—Great-Aunt Maiseen Billow, what a stroke! Every crack of the great Soltero's hooves on the dingy asphalt of Tenth Avenue had passed through his forehead like a shot. He confessed to me later that while he lay there on his back he had a vision of the Louisiana match horse, sailing through the air on a crane pulley, fully saddled, snorting high above the gray pleated wash of the harbor, into plumes of factory smoke, past the waist of the steamer and down to the deck again, like a rising and a setting sun.

"Just remember in your application to the Ox Roast committee to ask for the breakfast speaker's slot—believe me, at 7 a.m. the Curare Society will still be struggling out of their sleeping bags. And I positively guarantee with my topos you'll win money, brother Shipoff. Win, don't you hear!"

"Win," Shipoff repeated automatically. For what was it to shove a doped-up and colicky novice lector to the speaker's table, prop him up on the lectern and run for cover, just to collect two hundred grand at the finale? Was this threading his coils through the nostrils of Soltero? Was this leading Soltero off?

XVII
Three Masters

Dr. Analarge was in his laboratory tracking the Inexpressible; Shipoff lay on his pet bench, dreaming up unwritten Manuals on the S.C.O.R.; the World-Friar Tapsvine had a new chapel, and prepared to milk a "Waste Confession" every Sunday from our jaws. This was the Depot in its summertime, levels A, B, and "ground" atop the Hibernaculum. Below us the Pit hummed along with this activity, a sort of resonating cavity, like a larynx.

The tripod of my worldly masters was complete.

And as all human knowledge is imperfect but that which reflects on its own imperfection, so my education was doomed to fall short till the days my three masters bent their heads together in the council chamber, the better to take running butts at each other.

The first occasion was bloodless, the words bone dry. At the meeting where he was officially introduced, Tapsvine asked leave to bring his anaconda Nana to the Depot fold, pleading attachment, vegetarian habit and the infirmity of years…

Quot years? asked Analarge, who loved this sort of garbage, making some sort of calculation on his clipboard.

800/824…

Secundum?

Secundum! Shipoff swivelled around bleary-eyed in the chairman's seat. Secundum!

Tapsvine said: Thanks to radio-carbon analysis on middle strata Mundurucu mother mollifiers, slate feet unmistakably pointed to aft, removed from her intestinal tract during exploratory surgery.

That revealed? said the doctor.

O, nothing more alarming than those interesting but indigestible objects, now in the Growth and Tumor Collection of the World-Friar's Museum.

Tapsvine bowed and sat down. Shipoff sat staring at his pencil, ignoring the hands in the air. Eight hundred years! he said at last. Eight hundred years! And how does she get around, by coiling herself around her wheelchair?

The assembly tittered, and the doctor labored to his feet, perspiring solicitously:

Respected colleague Tapsvine, assume the tests are reliable, and the mother mollifiers are as old as you say. All the same, why couldn't the specimen have licked up the artifacts from the rubble of some perished Mun...duh...

Mundurucu, Tapsvine said.

Mundurucu settlement in the Panhandle—just last year?

Tapsvine snapped back: E-strata, brother doctor, twenty feet down.

Then Shipoff: Well, how about just last year from the pocket of some E-strata Mundurucu archaeologist, as alarmingly uninteresting as he was digestible?

The house laughed.

In all earnest, said the doctor with embarrassment, it's not that I question eight hundred. But why only eight hundred? Why not sixteen? Or even twenty-four? Why shouldn't the specimen have lived 800 years before lapping up her first Mun...duh...Mun...duh...mollifier, especially since she went the next 800 without polishing off another one?

Tapsvine ignored this till the doctor sat down. He then announced: By your leave, mister chairman! This anaconda will live in retirement in the chapel-loft as my guest, as quiet as a mole and no nuisance to anybody.

Shipoff said: It's my Depot! This anaconda, with all due compassion for her infirmity of years, will live down the hole in the Hibernaculum, or nowhere.

The hole or nowhere. On this point the World-Friar yielded. Nana went down the shaft. But from now on when a master sipped the fountain in the Concourse meeting hall, the burble at the head was Meribah.

Then one night in the middle of May, Fraulein Analarge sent a pair of bloodhound bitches over the Sump and gave them the run of the Depot. Her father and loyal slave the doctor hastened to assure the tripodial council that the olfactory bulbs, fila, and hippocampal formations of these monsters with teaspoon brainpans were congenitally insensitive to the vertebrate male, whom they registered as simply a mineral conglomerate, a sort of walking rock. On the other hand the dogs had been bred and trained, blood and bone, for the methodical tracking and dismemberment of women.

It was for this refinement of their natural tendency that Annie introduced the bitchhounds to the Depot. A precise and lengthy description of the dogs, as well as a delivery timetable, was humanely posted in the Depot duplicating department well in advance of their actual arrival. Consequently the entire Anti-Annie Analarge League, with Yeeza at the head, holed up in the Depot duplicating bunker, where they had time to lay in two weeks' victuals. Although their powerfully worded petition on the issue lay under Shipoff's gavel in the Concourse chamber, an anonymous lobbyist had already pointed out to each member, in little flyers each of which held a crackling $20 bill, how a delicate silence reigned nowadays in the upramps on summer afternoons, and how, in the Depot dump, crickets could be heard...

The vote that followed made it plain that a temporary loss of its associated female population would be taken with good cheer by the Topical Tropists, masters and lectors alike. The tripodial council quietly tabled the petition for fifteen days, at which time the promptings of decency brought AUNTY's case back under discussion. The council quickly voted to dispatch another two weeks of canned beets and chicken chow mein to the ladies of the duplicating department, packed into the dumbwaiter in so many two-pound cans.

One would think that Fraulein Analarge would have been happy to coast for a spell after such an easy win. But no, on the contrary. At the second Depot council after they were delivered, the doctor slavishly introduced the Vive-Annie Analarge Party's three-point plan for the bitchhounds, as follows:

1. *Council Endorsement*
2. *Cultural Enhancements*
3. *Grassroots, then Official, Deification*

By Chrust, it was embarrassing. The doctor slid a color photograph of Annie and kennel under the opaque projector, and fell to his knees.

"I see these dogs as in a dream, I revere them from racial memory as the archpriests of the medical profession. Gentlemen, as we have tunneled into earth for our Hibernaculary spa, so the hounds of Aesculapius's daughter now rise to the Depot groundworks, from Inexpressible depths!" The doctor's plump palms shook on the projector, transmitting a volcanic tremor to the image on the wall.

The snapshot blown up there little needed amplification. It had been snapped from foot level, so that Annie shot up like a giantess between bitchhounds, with her clonic hairdo lost in the treetops. Beside each plantessimal kneecap in mid-stride was a dog's open jaw, a tongue dangling out of it as incongruously pink and huge, in that perspective, as a baboon's ass.

At the top of her legs, curling out of her tunic, was a blueblack corkscrew of pubic hair from her celebrated *mons veneris*. This was cheesecake, a lure for the indifferent, and a bone to obstinate dog haters.

But the bait was lost on Shipoff. Moreover a freak of genetics turned his boredom into violent recoil.

With respect to Sergei Shipoff, leading lectromagnate of Big

Yolk and the Americas, the male-insensate faculties of Fraulein Analarge's bitchhounds were scoring only about .500. With the Anti-Annie Analarge League safely locked and barred in the duplicating bunker, the bored dogs sniffed around Shipoff in an ominous way. And then as a Pennsy pinky to the average dog where rabbits have disappeared from the landscape, so stood Shipoff to the bitchhounds, in the absence of an actual female population.

By and by one morning, without actually breaking the skin, they chased him up and down the Sumpsky Prospect till he crawled, chewed his houndstooth pantscuffs beyond recognition, exposed his small toupee to the world, and frightened him out of his wits. Fraulein Analarge was in Big Yolk for the afternoon, probably shoplifting up and down Park Avenue. The lectromagnate mustered a recoil of the cataplectic school—overshot, for the bitchhounds' attack was recreational, not carnivorous. Doctor Analarge waved his arms and shouted frantically, but the bitchhounds were deaf to suggestions from mineral conglomerates.

Finally Shipoff rolled back one eye and glorified the other. This stopped the puzzled bitchhounds just long enough for him to catch an aspen branch and yank himself out of danger.

They had cost him an oculomotor performance—number two! And where was Tapsvine all this time? The World-Friar, in spite of his famous successes with jungle carnivores, was not in sight—in fact he was perched the whole time on his chapel-loft window seat, nose pressed to the gutter pane. Here he sat roaring and hee-hawing at the lectromagnate's trials, taking in the action with a Bolex full of film.

A few days later, the explanation for the World-Friar's absence during the assault reached Shipoff from Wally's Billiard Parlor in West Poolesville, where Tapsvine had premiered the reel with the regular Wednesday night smokers.

Reprisals were due all around.

"From Inexpressible depths!" the doctor repeated. "And what more proper Hygeiea, what more natural hostess to this therapeutic mineshaft, our Depot cum Hibernaculum, than my adored Yanneleh, herself the deep pit of womanly hygiene?"

Now the doctor was no wind-bag. In fact it was the sheer simplicity of his excesses that passed what Tapsvine could endure.

"Really, Dr. Analarge. A scholar, a physician and a ten-cent go-for! You let that bitchhound your daughter spoon-feed you that Aesculapian dog-shit, just so she'll hang around your laboratory for an afternoon."

Of all people, Shipoff rose to disagree. Short of actually confronting the bitchhounds face to face, there was nothing he wouldn't do now to thwart the World-Friar for taking those pictures. "The bitchhounds belong in the canon," he announced. "I'm for stuffing them both in the name of the profession. They'd look swell on those twin gumball-machine posts in the World-Friar's chapel..."

Now, between these pedestals, as Shipoff well knew, the World-Friar Tapsvine hung his jungle hammock, the better to flick his cigarette butts into the holy water while he watched the Late News from Big Yolk.

"Stuff them!" cried the doctor in terror. "*Rachmones*! She'd kill me."

"Now there's the primitive religion I yearned to feel in the early days," Tapsvine said. "Quite respectfully, Analarge, why not keep the dogs and stuff her?"

The doctor was in tears.

"There now, she treats you like a dog, *nicht wahr?*" Tapsvine yawned, then said loudly, toward the lectern:

"No Analarge bitchhounds in my chapel, period."

Shipoff sneered back, "O no?"

Finally Doctor Analarge blew his nose and rocked to his feet, taking the floor. "*Fech!* The church went to the dogs, Brother Tapsvine! Why not let the poor dogs go to church?"

The World-Friar sat down in disgust.

"Make faces, I don't care," cried the doctor. "Were you there? I was there. Little porks, I've seen things you've never seen in places you'd never dream, whence the state of my mind..."

(Bravo!) (Do it to me!) The novices cheered satirically.

"Nor can a state be empty but reels on and on, and you know it's a man's duty to reel on if he can't stick to the point without frying on it. Then his life is like a movie reel, it can't come on without going by at the same time, even on the rewind. So I'm a ten-cent go-for, but even truckdrivers cry at the movies.

"I came to light in the French Hospital in Smyrna, *belle infidelle Smyrne,* on the October cusp I share with the likewise symphoniac doctors Browne and Coleridge, in 1908. I'm the son of a doctor, son of the same, back to Galen himself—I'm what they call a Levantine Jew, but of Kurdish-Armenian abstraction through a buby's buby, with one bastard outpost of Krishnamurtian aunts, plus the late Metropolitan of Smyrna for a godfather.

"I confess I was born with a Personality; and what a Personality it was! It was religious in face, I was a Jew who loved Chrust while Chrust lasted, not just Chrust but the whole string of them, for the whole megillah I have wept too much! At the first snort of incense I went down like one shot, when the muezzin bawled, when saints rode by and at *yontov* I flattened—so picture me at age twelve, a Personality and a fanatic, sore as a boil from assorted prostrations, my nose on the road to its present quashed point thanks to unrelieved poundings on the arcade sidewalk, from rolling on my belly towards Mecca, Llhasa, Nazareth or wherever, my forebrain a garble of laud in three languages, even throwing myself on the *caddesi* at the tinkle of the glacé pushcart...

"What a god was the god of my Personality, little porks. He had more routines up his snort than a snake oil vaudevillian.

"*Fech!* self-indulgence. I was due to be burnt out at twenty, a universal believer, an indiscriminate fanatic, a Personality! But Providence looked out for me, I was liberated, that's right, liberated in the Liberation. O still I praise god a little here a little there when I think of quitting my old hometown. I can't get it up like I could then. But who can?

"A little self-indulgence! I was even converted in a camp tent in Tulsa last August while Harfanger cackled...the old brain slipped a gear back to Paul of Tarsus, he copped a lectern in Izmir in his day. I mixed him up with this drugstore cowboy at the pulpit, one eye on the tent flap for a hasty exit, the other on heaven for flying vegetables, his pockets stuffed with bus schedules and hair-raising testimonials...

"I saw sea salt on those nose whiskers! He already stank like a camel. I fell on my knees! His flunkey sidled up with the pill bottles: 'Where does it hurt, pop?' I said, Little pork,

> *Hath he himself that is not sure?*
> *His trust is like as he hath sped...*

"Then I looked at the label. *Polycarp's Compound!* What does that stuff cure? 'Hemorrhoids, arthritis, warts, psoriasis, elephantiasis, excema, obesity, insomnia, urinary frequency, nuptial impotence and female problems. What do you have, pop?' I said All of them! Miscellaneous complaints too numerous to mention! You forgot your bottle, son! Wait, hear me out! I am hospitable to my diseases! For all I know they have the vote. Who is to say whether, but for the grace of these parliamentary microbes, there I went carted off to the crematorium? What if they voted me out of existence? In fact I'm not sure I vote against that ...

"Getting back to the hometown remedy, you know Marcus Aurelius himself came to Izmir across Smyrnoeus Sinus with a *vershlepteh krank.* The emperor was no whiner, but he thought it politic to roll up the coast to Pergamum to take the cure in the Asklepion. Now there was medicine! The Bosky Point Speedway Funhouse, a quickie car wash and the Big Yolk Tunnel on the Grand Sump Line have nothing on that operation. The emperor ran down the sinkhole while the priests spouted their regular hocus pocus through the ceiling vents. All this the emperor endured with justice, and remembering Epicurus, smiled without sweating at the great physicians perched on the ledges with their leeches and purges, laxatives, drastics and pills. One smiled back!—a bird of a man who held out a legume bouquet, sworn to by the best gladiators. He was Galen. Marcus took him to Rome, but back home his sister married an Analarge.

"We're approaching the modern era! While yet I had a Personality to prostrate, I laid my short pants in the gutter of the Rue Jaune, a spit off the Anafartalar Caddesi, the market street near the customshouse in the Jewish quarter. Yellow roses twisted over the streets there on wires between balconies, the dust was full of petals. And grapevines grew on the courtyard trellises, silvered with tiny hairs. A lovely town! And over the arbors British shells salted the sky with stars from the harbor to Mt. Pagos, while the whole city watched from the rooftops, tinkling *politakia* in honor of the Great War, their usurious nephews making a killing in camp chairs on the quay...

"But at tea time when the *imbat* from the harbor died down, an exotic odor used to fill the air—it was a million and a half corpses of the race of Ararat, some buried, some not. It was 1922. I was liberated when Ataturk liberated the fatherland, backing the foreign infidel off the hometown docks. All the Armenian mamas, expecting to have their bellies slit, their clits hacked off and their babies skewered, were jumping like circus fleas into the Bay of Smyrna from the seawall while the city burned behind them. *Fech!* They burned Smyrna down just to clean her up; there were more corpses than dogs to eat them.

"In the midst of the festivities the Bey, a man of terrific, resplendent Personality, carried away with good nature, made a personal present to the folk: the old Smyrniote Metropolitan Chrysostomos, my godfather, fond of his dinner! a scant five feet with a mouth, alas! as big as his beard, both reeking of garlic and Metaxa, with a partiality to Christians and a fatal interest in politics, which crept into his sermons at embarrassing intervals. They pushed him down Anafartalar Caddesi as far as the shop of Ismail the Italian hairdresser, they tied him in Ismail's apron, tore out his beard and the skin with it, popped his eyes out, cut his ears and nose off with Ismail's razor, and kicked him, still living, as far as the Namazgha quarter, where they cut him in four pieces and left him for the dogs.

"After all, porkpies, he was the last Metropolitan of the last of the seven churches of Asia—for him the dogs made room. So you see it's a fact that the church went to the dogs in the latter days, and he was no blueplate special either, that cantankerous old Personality of a Metropolitan, much less on a full stomach.

"As for me, I was put on a packet to Salonika and I haven't been back. No doubt that was where I left my Personality. Twenty-five miles offshore you could see the fire that cured it in the midnight cloud banks... ."

The doctor stopped to light his fat perfecto. The fragrance of Transylvanian woodlands filled the chamber, as if to say, *Deigeh nisht!* Don't worry! I know how to be persuaded to the side of the living and to take my comfort. "So you never heard the one about Izmir, little porks. Well, each bloodbath washes over the last. You never slurp the same soup twice, and you always get something new to talk about over dinner. There's a convention behind that howl MARTYR, the howl has a use, a biology, like a belch, to break up the long seder of slaughter, to crack up into courses the feast, *fech!* there are no breaks in killing. But such is the power of words, to push a hearse up the tracks, loaded with praising, nor can a word be empty but it's all praise except the accurate silence of the corpse, the man who knows better than to live..."

The assembly of lectors was bored. Balls of paper sailed through the air toward the Concourse skylight. Candy wrappers crackled, peanut shells crunched under foot. Chin in his hands, Shipoff snored into the mike on the lectern, like a small outboard motor trying endlessly to turn over. Only Tapsvine rose and applauded the doctor. They turned and bowed to each other like men of the world of a hundred years before.

"Doggedly argued."

"*A shainen dank.*"

"I concede the point, doctor. The bitchhounds belong in the chapel-loft—stuffed."

"After all this!" cried Dr. Analarge. "*Gait, gait.* My daughter would kill me."

"I'll have a word with Fraulein Analarge…"

Sure enough, a week later the two bitchhounds stared down from twin poles beside Tapsvine's confessional, in lifelike poses, out of red glass eyes.

XVIII

13 Days Pre Ox Roast

The World-Friar was lying at his ease, and so I asked him:

"What did you mean, telling Shipoff he didn't have to stick his neck out 'either' at the Ox-Roast?"

He was sprawled in the hammock smoking one of his Suez brand cigarettes, his face full of pleasure, watching fat clouds roll down the summer sky through the open gutter window.

He tapped off an ash, which zoomed blindly around the holy water basin once or twice before it sank. "I meant he should avoid a bullet in the head. It isn't healthy, little brother."

That's what I thought he'd meant. My chin sank down to my hands on the altar. This was the closest I had been to a lectern in months. But for weeks sleep had been eluding me because of that suggestion of Tapsvine's to the lectromagnate, that ended in *Use a proxy*. And though I seemed at last to see a lit-up lectern in the offing, it was one lit up with combat flares, pitted with grapeshot and shrapnel, a bullet hole clean through just at the level of the heart, and poisoned arrows sticking out of it all over, like porcupine quills.

The Ox Roast was only 13 days away. Though handbills were turning up everywhere with *Shipoff's Topical Tropists* inserted next to "Hibernation Hindthoughts" in the Midsummer's Day breakfast program, Shipoff had yet to name the lector for the occasion. Neither had anyone volunteered, but no one looked worried. After all, whenever a grade B lector had been needed in the past to titillate, puzzle or distract lay observers, the choice had always been Shamp.

I could hear them thinking it. True, my ear wattles were cut off, and I had the World-Friar's friendship, possibly protection. Still, no sleep. Only those whom bad luck has ignored trust luck. Those whom bad luck zeroes in on once or twice feel shiny ever after in its eye, like chrome knobules.

To subvert these reflections, I eased them into a journal. The first entry, undated, involved a paltry scrap of calculus along Shipovian lines:

QUERY:

Where would wisdom have recoiled?
What revision would suffice to deposit
his luckless ass (HS) miles from present
*   conjunctions?*

Luckless Ass (-Brakeknot) = Shipoff + (Analarge [-Annie]) + W-F Tapsvine

$$HS = 0(OR)$$

HS = home safe

0(OR) = No Ox Roast

HS from hindthought: Defeat of Brakeknot

Why I ever let him get away?
How I let the old crust hang me up on definitions?

Why when he asked what I'd been 15 minutes past, I didn't ask what he'd be 15 minutes hence, stuff in fuse & 2-ounce powder charge, blow him and gravestone to East Gopher Landing?

12th DAY PRE OX ROAST

Nights are cool in the chapel-loft, on the deck of the gutter window. Never slept but came to, this a.m., to the World-Friar swinging a corked vial of clear fluid in the sunlight. "In order to hump Miss Brakeknot economically and fast, administer one half of odorless contents in gin, tea, or vanilla malted; beware of chocolate, which produces a blue precipitate."

"Talking in my sleep, eh?"

"It's not your sleep I'm worried about, it's mine. If you want to keep sacking out in my chapel, you'd better ball Miss Brakeknot and get it over with."

Explained Brakeknot as the prehistoric croaker whose belligerent influence got me into this stew.

"O well. Stew is the price of your inclusion in nature. If you make it till next week, Providence is everywhere..."

If I make it till next week, little stewballs of Brakeknot everywhere.

11th DAY PRE OX ROAST

Tapsvine in Big Yolk, hocking stuffed bitchhounds.

As soon as he fades down the Sumpsky Prospect this a.m., Shipoff sends for me, inflicting great terror. Lectromagnate lying on divan next to little electric fan. Agitation re true identity of larcenous Great-Aunt Maiseen has run its course. Appearance: leached out. Gin bottle on gum machine. Few days' growth of beard.

"I've lost you to the World-Friar," he says.

"You've been doing everything in style to lose me since New Year's."

"This is different from feeding you to the lady of my choice, the better to get us all fed." Drinks. "O Hughby Hughby. It's time I did some serious hibernating..."

What!

"I can feel a mortal slip-up ahead, coming round the mountain..." Shakes his head, swizzling gin-&-? in cup with little finger. "Don't know what, could be anything. Just up there around the bend..."

I say: "You can't do that. If you go down the hole now, the Big Yolk papers will say you didn't have the balls to introduce your own lector at the Ox Roast." Translation: If I'm going to get it, by Chrust they'll get a shot at you too.

He agrees! "You've stumbled on it, a bullseye for you, Hughby. What I have in mind is to blow a few kisses to the ladies, bow down to my hucklebones, and without ever standing erect again, dive down the hole before any of those chumps can get a sighting on me. Then I'll have a little vacation…"

Hearty congratulations for this idea. Behind paper cup, eye of the lectromagnate narrows a little on first and worst-loved lector, Hughbury Shamp.

Doubt revives. "Get up there by yourself, Sergei? A one-man bit? Just you?"

"Just me? Of course just me. Shipoff is enough! All you have to do, Hughby, is raise the hatch." A pause. "From the underside."

"No topos? No lectern?"

"No topos for Chrussake! Wear a gag and a demolition helmet if you want. Just get the hatch up on cue!"

What is sleep?

10th DAY PRE OX ROAST

"OX ROAST BLUES"

Thinking bout the city
I started walking down the track

Said I was thinking bout the city
Start to walk on down the track

Got to thinking bout the Ox Roast
Turned round came walking right on back

Dr. Analarge stormed chapel-loft at breakfast wearing nothing but his bedroom slippers. Distressed about empty bitchhound poles. Fraulein Analarge, *enceinte comme une vache*, missing from Depot grounds since last Tuesday. We deny all connection. Doctor pounds altar under my chin. While he pounds, Tapsvine pumps his butt with goofer hypodermic.

Dr. Analarge locked in former pay toilet.

An historic day.

WASTE CONFESSION INTRODUCED AT DEPOT

W. Poolesville Depot (June 15): At the sixth tripodial council meeting of Topical Tropists, Inc., today, the World-Friar Tapsvine introduced a program for intracommunity religious reform and standardization, whose outstanding topos is the requirement of Waste Confession.

The bill was passed unanimously after brief adulatory remarks by key Tropists, and was signed into effect by tripodial council chairman and Depot founder Sergei Shipoff at 3:00 p.m.

The World-Friar Tapsvine told newsmen in a brief statement this afternoon that he foresees an immediate popular response to the system, with "ultimately profound and far-reaching spiritual effects on society, beyond the Depot."

According to the official statement, the essential topos of the reform package are as follows:

1– The Sunday Sabbath is maintained.

2– Sunday services are instituted, attendance obligatory.

☞ Suggested weekly donation: 4 bits.
Absentees pay double.

3– A short sermon will be read.

4– A two-hour lunch break will be kept, to be held out on the Sumpsky Prospect, weather permitting.

☞ Bring your own booze.

5– WASTE CONFESSION is instituted. Effective immediately, there shall be universal public Waste Confession in the chapel every Sunday afternoon, with possible supplementary sessions on weekdays, as necessary.

W.C. EXPLAINED

According to Tapsvine, The Waste Confession is a culpafuge, a ritual device instituted to eliminate waste guilt from the metabolism of a peaceful and homogeneous community whose moral secretion is superfluous. The World-Friar told newsmen, "This is a simple system. It is comparable to the old British regulars draining their war wounds once a week, when some of those old Tommies couldn't remember if they got it in the Punjab or the Crimea."

An allegation by the Re-Natured Reasoning Study Group of Big

Yolk that his plan would foster "moral invalids" was emphatically denied by the controversial independent cleric, whose unorthodox proposals have caused consternation in conservative and liberal religious circles alike. He added, "We are concerned with essentially healthy individuals…who carry about little closed factories of moral infection because nature is sloppily retentive. We cannot pull the teeth of this venerable adaptation, but we can milk its venom… Waste Confession (is) an experiment in confessional fiction."

The ritual consists of the computation and recital, by each member, of the week's "crimes" against the community.

HANDBOOK FOR SCORING THE WASTE CONFESSION

CAUTION: DO NOT COMMIT THESE CRIMES!		
PECCANCY TABLE		DIRECTIONS
Treason & Desertion	6	I M P O R T A N T !
Intra-Depot Homicide	5	DO NOT COMMIT THESE CRIMES.
Unremunerated Blabbing,		IT IS DANGEROUS AND
Welshing on Gin Debts	4	UNNECESSARY TO COMMIT
Conspiracy To Seize Power		THESE CRIMES PRIOR TO
(House-Father Syndrome)	3*	CONFESSION.
Small-Time Bribery, Rake-		EVERY NOVICE LECTOR IS
Offs, &c.	2	EXPECTED TO ACHIEVE
Malingering, Petty Theft	1	MINIMUM PECCANCY* AT HIS
		FIRST CONFESSION.
REPEAT: DO NOT COMMIT THESE CRIMES!		
*Minimum Peccancy: 3		

INSUFFICIENT PECCANCY

Upon leaving the chapel loft the insufficiently peccant lector receives a card:

> (First Offense)
> Your peccancy was _____
> SUGGESTION: Drink more next week
> -
> (Second Offense)
> Your peccancy was _____
> A STRENUOUS EFFORT ON YOUR
> PART TO MARSHAL A HOUSE-FATHER
> SYNDROME FOR CONFESSION IS ADVISED
> -
> (Third Offense)
> Your peccancy was _____
> Your appointment with the World-Friar is:
> _____ at _____a.m.
> p.m.
> Your essay topic (500 wds.) is:
> *(Mail fraud, anal eroticism, &c.)*

Tapsvine is pleased with himself.

No sleep for two weeks.

8th DAY PRE OX ROAST

Hot evening, full of smoke. The aspen tops from the gutter window look like coils of dark smoke dotted with sparks— thousands and millions of lightning bugs. I hear a crackling: a raft poles up the Sump, parting cattails, bending little river birches out of the way…

A raft poles up the Sump? A bad sign. Hot air on sleep-starved eyeballs? There was never a raft on the Sump! Something about that bilge inspires a critical intelligence in the lowliest. Even muskrats trot down to the West Poolesville Bridge to get to the Big Yolk bank…

All the same I run to the bank and peer up the Sumpsky Prospect. And fading off in the river haze is a, a country official propped on his flagpole?—and, yes, a certain familiarly… vacant…sag in his britches bottom…

7th DAY PRE OX ROAST

Brakeknot in the vicinity.

Sat up this a.m. to the sight of his skinny moons stuck to the gutter window. Disappeared in the berry bushes.

L E C T O R S   A R E   H U N G R Y was painted by an anonymous lector in giant red letters on the wall of the Concourse chamber this morning in the pre-dawn hours. General address by Shipoff. Plea for solidarity in adversity. Predicts McCorkle will come through with household allowance by Friday… assures victory at Ox Roast…extends invitation for all the ox they can eat under semi-combat conditions to stronghearted lectors…no volunteers for breakfast slot…

Chow line at Analarge laboratory at 2:00. Bending with dipper over punchbowl I saw Brakeknot's waxy leer floating there among the orange peels. Whirling, threw punch across floral forecurls of entire Anti-Annie Analarge League, turned out in party dresses. Dipper raised lump on right temple of Alto Grizzard. Intended apology thwarted by mouthful of cheap hotdog, that antique saw should be fulfilled:

> My mouth is enlarged
> over my enemies.

By then, Brakeknot out of sight.

3:00 p.m.—Doctor Analarge cheered for munificence by crowd outside pay toilet.

Sleep impossible.

6th DAY PRE OX ROAST

Dr. Analarge released from pay toilet.
Tapsvine in Big Yolk bailing out Annie.

(clipping)

DAUGHTER OF SOCIETY M.D. NABBED

Big Yolk (June 17): The daughter of a well-known Big Yolk physician was arrested today in a West Side condominium, as she allegedly attempted to collect a tuition deposit for a nonexistent "chubbies'" diet-ballet camp in West Hinnstead.

Police have in custody Annie "Fraulein" Analarge, 27, daughter of Dr. Harry Analarge, a plastic surgeon who numbered many Big Yolk socialites and celebrities among his patients before his recent retirement, due to long illness, to a West Poolesville lectors' community.

The arrest was made by a plainclothes policewoman posing as an overweight housewife.

The suspect reportedly is also being held for questioning in connection with a fraudulent sale of subscriptions to an island weight-reducing holiday for singles last December, which led to the eight-day exposure of 18 persons without provisions on a mosquito-infested island in Galveston Bay.

A possible link to the recent disappearance of a busload of 14 seventh-grade girls on their way to a free beach party, later traced to a white slavery ring in Tarudant, Morocco, is also being investigated.

The attractive blond suspect, a professional soloist apparently several months pregnant, has denied the charges.

Wirephoto of Annie on courthouse steps. Also Brakeknot in lower left-hand corner, selling tamales.

No announcement on breakfast slot lector.

Still no sleep.

5th DAY PRE OX ROAST

As the soap bar said to the River Sump: Truth is a bubble on the stream. It's hard to be shore.

Litorally?

Would I tallow lye?

It's hard to be sure.

No sleep for weeks!

4th DAY PRE OX ROAST

Sleep, who needs it? Into the teeth of the Ox Roast, insomnia plunked this windfall: my 21-point Waste Confession, in which Brakeknot is defeated.

THE PASSAGE THROUGH CONVENTIONAL ORDEALS

Tapsvine refused my confession, he has popped me in the windpipe these three times.

1—"First thing in the morning, little brother."

2—"Shut up till sun-up or I'll tie you to the gutter window."

3—"Screw till daylight, Shamp, or by Chrust I'll hang you from the gutter frame—"

("But 21 points—")

"—gagged."

Temporarily suspended from the window lock, gagged. Writing arm going to sleep. Where might Tapsvine have picked up a pink silk brassiere marked A.A. that tastes like

(The journal ends here.)

XIX

My Waste Confession

When my eyes opened the sun was over the gutter window: it was noon. I had slept very well! The World-Friar had managed to slip the gag out of my mouth without waking me. The pink brassiere (if it was one) was out of sight. In the daylight perhaps it had looked less than kind between my jaws.

In a moment I remembered where I had left off. "Ready, Tapsvine?" No answer. Was he at Wally's? At lunch in the lectors' lounge?

No, a filament of pink smoke from one of the World-Friar's Egyptian fags was weaving in and out of the confessional box.

"Brother Tapsvine, I wish to Waste-Confess. Twenty-one points of sin I have sinned. Surely that's a Depot record?

"And as long as it's light out, could you get me down from this window hook? I'm sore as a boil in the pits…" I kicked the wall. No answer. All the same every second or two, a typewriter rapped off a volley behind the W.C. screen, like an Ox Roast terrorist stashed in the bog grass.

"Twenty-one points of Waste Confession—"

"Suck off, Shamp, I'm miles at sea…" He cursed softly over the space bar.

"At least get me down."

A book banged shut and he stuck his head around the corner of the chancel. The altar candles leapt from under my feet to float in his tiny eyes like wicks. He was not smiling, and his collar was limp with sweat. "You're in luck, Hughby. You can audit my first pre-W.C. sermon. What's missing I want to know.

THERE IS NO HOME

Pting! (He spat into the holy water basin.)

> There is no home
> There is station only
> By station is switchsiding
> Blind switching we sin
> And we must have sin
> We roll upon sin
> For man being bound to labor, uh, born to blunder,
>   POX! bound to blunder...
> With sin we whine without expectations
>
> Spit at the fire
> Spark neath the wheel & blah blah blah
> Withal knowing full well
> We can't make a case of it

THERE IS NO HOME

"A pox!—born to labor, bound to blunder, *fsshh!*—should I give them back 'scant' expectations..."

"Tapsvine! Let me down." I pounded the gutter window-pane with my elbows.

"What are you doing on that peg, Shamp?" said the World-Friar absently. "No wonder you didn't hear a word..."

"The chrust! I'm a lector, shall you say and I not hear it? Can I hear and not wind it back? *THERE IS NO HOME* pting *there is no home there is station only by station is switchsiding blind switching we sin and we must have sin we roll upon sin for man being bound to labor uh born—*"

"Stop!" He crossed over, plugged my mouth with one hand and lifted me down with the other. "Run along, little brother. Chapel's closed early today."

"You can't close the door on a 21-point—"

140

"Come on, Shamp, can't you contain yourself till Sunday? What a nag! a vice! repellent! it's an excess! The point of confessional fiction is not to scale the heights but to slide over the depths, to skate the old Pit without actually falling in..."

I waved the W.C. notice at him: "'With possible supplementary sessions on weekday afternoons, as necessary.'"

"Nothing is necessary." Nevertheless the World-Friar went back into the confessional, pulling his mustaches. A chair creaked under him. "Is it worth it? I might put you in a steel wool undershirt for this, Hughby."

I began.

"The basic peccancy is that I'm trying to sell the Depot out to the Adversary."

He snorted. "O no Hughbury, *c'est trop parfait*. They'll never believe this at Wally's. Wait a minute." (A *whirr*—a *hick*.) "Say it again for the tape recorder, go ahead..."

"First peccancy: trying to sell the Depot out to the Adversary. Treason. Score 6."

"Haw! haw!"

"With your permission—second peccancy: Homicide upon the Adversary. Score 5."

"Hold it," Tapsvine spoke up. "At least do it by the rules, Hughby. The Adversary what's-his-name, that humorous Grapenut, *nicht wahr*, the 'murdered' foe, is not at the Depot. Only intracommunity homicide is in the peccancy table."

"Correction: Brakeknot is at the Depot. He arrived on the grounds Monday night. Tuesday morning he pressed his naked buns against your gutter pane." And I pointed to the two egg-shaped blots on the glass—a light fur of skyblue mold had sprouted on them over the weekend.

The World-Friar said nothing.

"Brother Tapsvine, Sergeant Brakeknot is at least at the Depot—give me the benefit of the doubt."

"Five points," he allowed, squeaking back in his chair. "But little brother, you haven't killed him yet. And dead or not, that's only eleven..."

141

"Keep counting. This Brakeknot is an old tracker but he lacks experience of the city-solo. How should he know the lectors are starving, the tripodial council is at war with itself? Will a map leak the hazards of the Ox Roast? What does he know about the Arslevering wad? So, here's a body who has had a little fame of his own, who's obsessed with fame, who's going to pieces at its effortless boom all around him. His usual circumspection flies in all directions when he hears the name Arslevering dropped in connection with a breakfast lector's slot, and a cheap line or two from the Hibernation topos (Unremunerated Blabbing, score 4). He falls for that line! The old wolf lets himself down the well with it in one bucket, while the foxy Shamp who invited him down for a swim rides up in the other. In the end he gets my lectern at the Arslevering Ox Roast for a small fee (Small-Time Bribery, score 2), while I inherit his happy old age..."

"Not so fast. You don't have the breakfast slot to trade off. Shipoff is manning the lectern for a farewell wave, then KAVROOM, down the hole..."

"Maybe so. Then as soon as Shipoff is in hibernation, what's to stop me from taking over? (House-Father Syndrome, score 3.) I'm already under the hatch. I call Brakeknot, wrap him in a lector's toga, pop him through the roof and pick him up at teatime, with a bucket, mop and pushbroom if necessary. Intracommunity Homicide *qua supra*. Peccancy points: 5. Now say the truth, Tapsvine, how's that for a total Waste Confession?"

"You're a point short."

Drat, so I was.

"Why don't you steal a little something?" said the World-Friar, yawning. "One of those gold foil laurel wreaths, for instance, that are always lying around the Ox Roast speakers' table. That's an easy point."

"No, it has no dignity."

"Dignity! I wasn't aware that deadly vice had wedged its way into the peccancy table..." He began toying with the bell on the typewriter carriage, *ping, ping ping.*

"Here we go—as soon as I push Brakeknot out to the lectern I drop the hatch on my finger and I'm off duty for the duration."

"One for Malingering—21 points." Tapsvine ran out of the chancel and threw me a kiss. "You're a natural, Hughby. Now run along." But when he saw my eyes burning and my cheeks aflame, he stopped, groaned and walked back into the box. After a while he said: "You're not going to execute that ridiculous scenario, Shamp!"

"I want to get a crack at him!"

"Your score is zero." A match struck and the rosy thread of smoke lazily reappeared in the wattle work. *"DO NOT COMMIT THESE CRIMES.* Now clear out! Zero! Say twenty-one aves, staring a roast ox in the asshole. What do you take me for, your manager? You give me a pain in the F.F.V.—in fact I'm putting my money on Brakeknot, at least he stays out of my hair while he plots your earthly extinction."

"I've hardly slept for weeks. After 21 points, I should be able to go home and sleep."

"THERE IS NO HOME," said the World-Friar.

"Then absolve me."

"Absolve you!" He laughed. "Little brother, that one went out with phlebotomy." He came out of the confessional in a dinner jacket, with his surplice slung over one arm and a rack of corked test tubes in the other. "Take one, take one." He plucked one out himself and stuck it over my ear. "This'll put you out all right. You'll sleep and dream!"

Then he blew out the altar candles and, leaning on a hand, flipped out the gutter window. I sat there on the windowseat gazing at his dust and at Brakeknot's butt prints. Still it had been a fine Waste Confession, 21 points by the World-Friar's own count. Brakeknot was mine. Let the Ox Roast!

With the dope over my ear, I slept a night and a day.

143

XX
Court-Depoted

I woke up in soledad, I had drifted and run aground. When did it rain? The Sumpsky Prospect stared back from a long string of puddles. Had I been snoring all day in the open window, and no one had called me to a class, a meeting, a plate of rice and chitlins?

That was cold. Colder yet, someone had snapped off my lector's collar and shirtfront while I slept, and left me to wake up in my BULIMY tee shirt.

Scratching my head, I went down to the lectors' lounge to have a bowl. And there in the Thousand Palms decor, no one would speak to me. A desert. The prairie chicken hearts of my colleagues strained to fade into cloudless blue wallpaper scattered with smoke trees and century plants...

Lambert Cauley loitered at the counter. "Volunteer for the Ox Roast breakfast spiel yet, old Cauley-Flower?" He snatched up his orange phosphate and rice ration and scuttled away to a table for one, making sure to plant his meal sack rearend solidly in my direction. The little camp chair creaked obstreperously underneath him—normally prudence confined old Cauley to barstools.

I carried my rice to the lectors' common table. A dozen novice lectors sat smoking, playing penny polo, aiming balled-up napkins at the wallpaper sierra tops.

"I'll join you handsome cowboys," I said, waving my utensils. "Speak to me!"

A few last pennies sailed through the air and skidded unplayed off the table edge. My colleagues sat silent, staring at the littered tablecloth.

I sang,

> Where seldom is heard
> A discouraging word…?

Nothing. I ate a little, but the chopsticks fell out of my hand. "Okay, what's the gaff? How about sharing your reveries on the morphology of yesterday's rice grains with your old pal Hughbury Shamp?" Nothing. "Then blow it out your assholes!" And I ran out of the room.

I went to my old phonebooth down the tube from the Concourse. The door was open a crack, but when I pulled it wider the air boiled into my face, hot as wilderness. The crusts of dying June beetles snapped under my shoe soles, a thousand lacewings and gnats zoomed over the ceiling light.

I composed my mind and crawled under the seat with the populace.

Hang it all!

Every dog follows his track to his day, and truly my day was always erect on the twilight horizon like a March hare on Leap eve, likewise off and running for Fool's Day at the first light of sunrise. This was understandable. This was a dog's life, properly so-called. But how had I managed to wake up one June day with not only my day but my dogdom called in question?—decollared, cast out, left to crouch in a ten-cent telephone booth with even the telephone out of order, the dead receiver bobbing on its cord by my ear like a vitrified fetus.

I must have done something…

Novice lectors, depot toadies and usherettes were collecting in agitated clusters in the Concourse. Then all at once Shipoff padded down the upramp in his crepe-soled summer cordovans. From under the seat I could only observe the lectromagnate from his waist down to his sixth toes, but that, earnest lector, was plenty. For caught up in his fist and wadded like a compress over his overworked liver were a lector's striped jacket and a pair of pink duck trousers—mine. So Beebee Borigard had kindly mailed them back to me in time for the Ox Roast along with his bill, remembering also to put them in care of the lectromagnate, all this to prove the ubiquity of the human heart, no doubt.

When Shipoff had paced the length of the Concourse he wheeled, and I perceived in his other fist one of those long pronged poles with which park attendants spear discarded paper plates and transit stubs...

"Out! come out, Hughby you mutt, I know you're here. You always pop out when the wind changes." He thrust the pole under each wooden bench in the waiting room, row after row. "You're being roundhoused, my little pint-boiler. Court-Depoted. Now come out and defend yourself like a lector."

He pushed each iron ashcan in the Concourse over after running it through a few times—the Depot flunkeys ran anxiously along behind him with pushbrooms. *Blang!*—he kicked open the steel-lined door of a utility closet and stabbed savagely at the mopheads. He even jerked up the wooden blind to the center shaft and unhitched the dumbwaiter, which bombed down eight levels and bounced in the casing on the Pit floor like a cannonball, *kapploong, kapploong, kapploong.* A block of tiles fell out of the ceiling, powdering a few heads. Meanwhile the entire Topical Tropist confederation seemed to be arriving, including the doctor's band. Tapsvine and Analarge hurried in simultaneously from side exits. And now in they filed, the comrades who wouldn't talk to me in the lectors' saloon...

I had mixed feelings about the turnout. True, they were interested in old Shamp, but only to see him carved up into steaks and trotters. "HUGHBURY!" Shipoff shouted, pounding the lectern, his hair sticking out wildly all but the little toupee, which lay like a peaceful isle in a sea of cattails.

The World-Friar promptly joined the lectromagnate. "Where is the rapscallion? Left, eh? I knew I liked something about that boy." He laughed. "Your silent treatment, Shipoff. Novel idea! Masterful! What a tactician."

"O shut up. SHAMP! Last chance. Come out and speak for yourself like a lector."

And when did a lector ever speak for himself? O no—had we been on speaking terms just then I had certainly replied to the lectromagnate—O no my dear Sergei, in my topos-encrusted heart I nonetheless know there is nothing more picayune than to make a speech. Lector or not, you cock your jaw and you're in there to explain, convince, confuse, confute, confound, connive—you're not omnipotent but opposed, dragging along with the late freight, doing a job—all very well for a living, but not on my day off.

"Examine the defendant, Dr. Analarge! Get his motives," Shipoff shouted.

"Examine him in absentia?" said the doctor, troubled. "That would strain to comprise an Inexpressible..."

"Never mind that, examine him."

The doctor scratched his ear.

"That wouldn't be any fun," said the World-Friar.

Shipoff turned his back on them. "Dr. Grizzard!" he called into the crowd. From the end of the room, Alto Grizzard crept a few inches closer to the lectern. "Examine the defendant!"

"Doctor" Grizzard of the hair oil satchel, whose "doctorial" credentials were so questionable he went to Analarge for aspirin...

"Examine the defendant. Ask him anything! Expose him!"

Grizzard raised a finger, and the pulpy cheeks brightened. "Ah yes! The tsecret parts exposed in full moon like so, unter kaiser greatcoat." And he daintily spread his jacket flaps. Tapsvine and Analarge looked at each other in bewilderment.

"Pox, this is fun after all," said the World-Friar.

"Start the examination."

Dr. Grizzard shuffled foot to foot, tweaked his sideburns, felt carefully through his pockets—no, even at the outer limits of obsequiousness there was no getting around it:

147

"How begin without patient?" He smiled weakly.

"I'll sit in for the hangdog," Shipoff said.

There were four, maybe five muttered protests in the house. I will say that Tapsvine swivelled around in his chair in amazement, and Doctor Analarge blew his nose irately. Meanwhile Grizzard pulled a hair oil applicating sponge out of his waistcoat pocket between tongs: "Say ah."

"What!"

In terror Grizzard swabbed the thing over his bifocals. "Smear for microscopic organists, where is one is a pillion..."

"His health is okay, skip that part. Ask him why he ever came with me."

"So...why went with Shipoff?"

"To get to Big Yolk, the city-solo."

"Wat was the big fixturation on Big Yolk?" No answer. "Why else went with Shipoff?"

"*L'avez-vous vu, ce que j'aime!*" said Shipoff grandly.

"You are magnificent," Tapsvine smiled. "All the same, in the interests of accuracy. He was losing a private war back home—somebody Greatnuts. So why not two wars for the fledgling born loser? Why not six? Why not seven and three-quarters? Thus he turned his face to Big Yolk."

"Did he like me," Shipoff whispered to Dr. Grizzard.

Dr. Grizzard leaned forward with a knowing smile on his beak. "Wassy fond of you?"

"That's backwards, no, never mind. Hughby had his points, yes, for an unclean dog of an oscillator."

"But you liked hem, no?"

"Shipoff? He had range, striking feats of hindthought." The lectromagnate dreamed off for a moment. "On the other hand a little went a long way."

"What's done is done," Doctor Analarge broke in mournfully. "The little pork, we kept him busy night and day withholding his forgiveness..."

Peculiar theory, I thought, as the dust spiders tracked over my hair and down my neck. But Shipoff ploughed on. "Let's get to the point." He shoved the wad of clothes across the lectern top. *"What was he up to bareassed at Bertolt Borigard's?"*

In the far pews, all the novice lectors hooted and snickered. Well what do you think he was up to! Haw! haw!

"Zehr gut. Wat is this, aii, self-explanatorizing." It was my left shoe plug, reeking of tinea. I remembered stuffing the hole with the two carbons of Dr. Analarge's diagnosis as I ran down the puddled tubes toward Dr. Borigard's.

"Give that here, I'll take that." Dr. Analarge seized and opened the moldy flimsies and quickly crumpled them back into balls. *"Fech!* self-indulgence, I'm getting what I deserve. How can I make it up to them...he can be my secretary! Just let my two children come home. With the *ainikel.* They have a home! So long as they stay with Papa, they won't want for a thing."

This meant that in spite of her fullblown pregnancy Annie must not have come back to the Depot. Whispers flew around the room: she had jumped bail. The poor doctor thought I was with her! Shipoff snatched up one of the diagnoses and read. "I don't get it."

"I sent him away!"

"O so what. Did you give him Beebee Borigard's name and address? Did you strip the lector's duds off his bum? Did you tell him to trade blowjobs with the Tropists' natural enemy?"

The doctor groaned on incoherently.

"No, I did it by myself," Shipoff cried, "I, Shamp, confess! Once I went with Shipoff, my life was a lectern in Big Yolk, the city-solo. But when the lectromagnate wasn't drooling in his cups he was dealing what few lecterns popped up in the early days to his 'starboy' of the moment. I personally saw fit to conserve my sweet asshole for less, O, tortuous insinuations. I knew Bertolt Borigard had a few oldtime lecterns on his rounds. An old stoker like Beebee, he would jump through hoops for a clean punk like Hughbury. So I went in and had him cut off the ear-bobs Shipoff loved so much—snip, snip—you should see the bill he sent me—but while I was still casing out that money-grubbing old plug I got wind that the World-Friar Tapsvine was camped a few yards off in the Great Morass—so I got off a good thing to—"

"I personally cut those ear-wattles off," Tapsvine announced. "What's worse, the ignoramus didn't know me till I introduced myself. And what's this *my life was a lectern in Big Yolk?* How can he be what he never had at all? He hardly got to Big Yolk much less to a lectern—you could as well call that patsy a telephone booth or a coupling pin as a lectern."

"Believe me," Shipoff cried, "it's those homeless coupling pins that are in the biggest hurry to sell their jockey shorts for the first topos that comes along. And I don't blame them! A readymade topos is the phonebooth of your reputation. All right! Let's get to the condemnation."

Dr. Grizzard stepped forward and spread his jaws happily, but Shipoff pointed him off the floor.

"I'll take care of this part! "Shamp! I know you're in here! We the tripodial council find you flit from one master to the other not omitting the extra-Depotial variety. We don't want you at our lecterns! But the World-Friar reminds me you have to have a lectern to lose one—well, here's the Ox Roast break-fast table slot…"

This was no surprise to me, in my telephone booth.

"…O you do have a choice, Shamp: either the Ox Roast lectern or—down the hole indefinitely! Roast or hibernate! but oscillate no more."

The lectromagnate retired with a flourish, leaving the groundskeeper's pole winging barbarously out of the lectern top.

A little respiratory crisis reigned in the Concourse, but the clapping, at first scattered, soon rose in waves, while the gasps were lost to history. The Anti-Annie Analarge League betrayed its enthusiasm by hooting, stomping and blowing up popcorn bags, I gather at the prospect of getting me back in the Pit. No shot, ladies! On the other side of the hall I saw Lambert Cauley hastily tearing up little pink and green slips—all my IOU's, the principal mementos of our buy-you-a-beer relationship. No doubt he was wondering if our casual connections would compromise his own future in the city-solo. Rest easy, old Cauley-Flower, that which a man has not, how can anyone take it away from him? But the face that dominated the Concourse chamber at the finale was that of the standard novice lector, clapping for his supper as Shipoff's stroganoff eye swooped down the hall: the face, nineteen times out of twenty, of an ectomorph, 17, 18, or 19 years old, fair-haired and a little bulgy-eyed, with a wide calm forehead, calm with gross relief.

I was calm myself. Safe with the spiders and earwigs I rolled back on my hams to watch an arctiid moth plink against the ceiling light and fall back stunned in the fifth round. I noted of the moth that while the intervals grew longer, the tropos never varied… Refrain from the metaphysical analogy, earnest lector, for it is vain. There was no more between me and that moth than between me and a Big Yolk lectern. Go by also the phonebooth and the coupling pin, for all these things do what they do and are what they are or nothing. As for me, who knew what I was? And by St. Cornwallis, who cared what I was, so long as I could herd my points and tracks, topos and indirections over the yawning gorge, and arrive in my skin one day post Ox Roast?

I was Shamp. I hoped in the doctor.

"*Fech*, I object," he was saying. "To traduce the little porkpie in his absence is bad enough—"

"He's here, I know the cagey punk," Shipoff said.

"—As for buggery, ridiculous! He loves my daughter. And a little lapse into treason? *Schver*, the punishment is too much. The Ox Roast is *schver*, but at least it's only an hour. But indefinite hibernation! it's a crime against nature."

"A crime against nature, haw!" Tapsvine slapped his knee. "That one went out with fichus and claret and the Felicific Calculus. Show me a crime against nature, Doctor Analarge, and I'll show you a frog that with a milligram of novocain eats his own froglegs, a goose that, fished out of the millpond, sidles up to a mirror and lays an egg. Nature is crime, eventually. She sins by inclusion. She causes the frog to get on the train and he stays on until he gets kicked off post mortem. His stop comes along:

TOOT TOOT! Bad blood!

He doesn't get off. He doesn't know how."

"*Fech*! she puts the poor frog on the train and goes on to muskrats, discouraging thought…"

"Show some guts, Doctor Analarge," said the World-Friar. "It's a free ride. At least it's a cheap ride. Little brothers, in trying to figure out what you're doing in that shiny three-dollar Fast Flying Vestibule you came to in, with all the little gauges, needles, ciphons, cogs, plugs, gears, pins, valves, hoses, vents and chrome knobules on the board, never put your money on the lizzie which transports you, for

its breath is a combustion

its track is a toil

its climb is a switchback on a parlous trestle

its descent a blind speedball devoid of judgment

its coupling unsure

its mileage a dream and folly of expectation

its destination: ZOOKER."

"Zooker," the house murmured, "zooker, zooker," compelled by some incantatory steam in the end syllables…

If you ever chance to hear him, earnest lector, you'll agree that the World-Friar didn't take up the altar (what was left of it) for nothing.

XXI

A Home

I waited on my belly to head Analarge off, in a rhombus of nasturtium and iris he had planted in front of his laboratory pre-fab. As I lay there I remembered the two green sponges he strapped to his pie-shaped knees in the fall and spring, and his delicate hand with a trowel, *whap whap whap*. I had a sudden longing to play with a shovel and green things...

Along came the doctor.

"Papa Analarge—" But he brushed by me without stopping, and I duck-walked along in his broad shadow lest some over-zealous lector coming out of the Court-Depot should look this way up the Prospect. "Papa Analarge, I'm home."

He pushed a big key into the mouth of the basilisk on the vestibule padlock, and white nylon laboratory walls snapped up around us. Then he slung his jacket over the counter, sat down and his head sank into his arms. "O Hughby. The sooner you bring her home the better. Get married tomorrow, you have my blessings." He banged the table. "If only I didn't have this kasha with the Floricomous, I could see it Inexpressibly..."

The Floricomous—this meant one of chez AUNTY, probably Yeeza, was renewing old ties with the doctor. "So Aunty Ames comes around when Annie's away...?"

"*Fech!* the minute she sees my daughter cross the Sump she ploughs through that door. Into my house!" The doctor grabbed my forearm. "She would raise the hair on a snake. Don't let her in!"

"Rest easy, Papa—" But I was spared the bravado. Even at that moment Yeeza Ames burst through the gargoyled vestibule padlock, past the two of us into the kitchenette.

The doctor stared into space. A grackle landed on the open laboratory window and he said to it with a futile whirl of the fingers: "The pantry door is open, Maximus. She only does that to intimidate me with her omnipotence."

So this was home, home with a master of the old masters. Sitting across from the doctor at the marble counter I observed that our conjunction wasn't the charge to my solar plexus it would have been half a year ago. In fact I wondered if Doctor Analarge would hide me at all, or would he insist I chew off the forkful Shipoff had landed between my teeth, to merge with the spirit without gagging. For all the masters used that clause when their charity was exhausted.

First there was the doctor's laughable idea that I had the power to lead Annie up one foot of the Sumpsky Prospect, much less across a cold subway floor to the upramp of matrimony. Not that the Hughbury I was now would be tempted to come between the fool and his error. But how long could the show go on without Fraulein Analarge putting in an appearance?

Secondly, beyond the uneternal aegis of this illusion lay policy. The doctor was more than a kind man: he was a just man, as men are just. That is to say, his liberality extended to his nerve endings, no farther. I strayed up the track of our future conversations, and ran into this engulfing ritornello—

1. You were very badly served…
2. Fight them to the end…!
3. But hide? My son, are you a cynic?
4. You're not planning to sleep in my pantry for the rest of your life…?
5. *Fech!* every man's life is sufficient.

(or)

154

It is horseracing. (The doctor might be strung along till one day post Ox Roast. And he might not.)

Dinner at four. The celery hearts, ribs of beef, the asparagus, the bread sticks, and finally Yeeza herself had all been trussed up for the occasion in painful-looking red elastic bands. Doctor Analarge turned to me with a wince: "Perhaps she means to say we are a bundle of faggots?"

"She's not so clever."

"I don't know."

The doctor ate everything on the table, including the center-piece, a wax red onion. Then he shoved himself back from the linen and said:

"Boeuf montmorency blah blah blah. Sauce perigourdine blah blah. Rose hips en gelee blah blah." He staggered to his feet, blew a fart, and went slowly up the rope ladder to the laboratory loft.

Yeeza and I watched each other over broken heaps of napkins. Presently there came from above one of those grand vitreous detonations that have a privileged place in stock re-hashes of the doctor's newsworthier eccentricities, sold to scandal magazines by his disgruntled former secretaries. From the force of this particular blast the north and west faces of the laboratory broke from their mortises, but owing to the box hedge the doctor had lately put in, didn't fall flat to the ground but rather hung out like portcullises. Green sulfurous fumes curled around the newly opened crack between loft and laboratory. Then I jumped up, thinking I heard flames crackle.

O it was all described with precision in an acrimonious exposé I had read in some monthly rag, sent in by one freshly fired secretary or another. It explained that whenever the doctor unpredictably tired of a piece of research he was engaged in, he would yank the fifth table leg and French café cloth out from under all the glassware in service just then in his upstairs studio, regardless of the pressure, volatility, odor, molecular stability of the contents. Afterwards any allusion to the recent blast in the doctor's hearing was a fatal blunder—a firing offense, one among hundreds. Only a light hand with a whisk-broom and pan were prescribed...

I looked at the waves of chartreuse gas rolling around the light fixture and studied the crackling in the upper story. By the long sober jaw and flat English ass of St. Cornwallis! what was it to add a little red fire extinguisher from the vestibule to the equipage, so long as I clasped the gadget discreetly under my armpit?

I had never been up to the loft before. Still dangling a corner of the French tablecloth, the doctor sat in an old armchair, the puffs of his perfecto exactly matching the flower balls on the maroon upholstery, as if those dingy chrysanthemums were somehow percolating up his anus and intestinal tract and out the end of his cigar.

He was turning pages of his notebooks, and he did not look up.

"Darling Anneleh, your papa knows he's been neglecting you. But wait till you hear the idea I had. *Shaineh* Yanneleh, think of Sirius B, the midget twin of the Dog Star, such a runt compared to old Hotshot, all the same we know that a tea-spoon out of this petzeleh weighs a ton. A ton down to a teaspoon now! And of the Old Dog himself! It strains to com-prise an Inexpressible, a point made all.

"Self-indulgence, Yanneleh. Your loving father, after all these years, the old fart is stuck with a Personality. But now he proceeds toward the point by measures, with wisdom, by the teaspoon. At the last moment he gives the old cesspool the space of a test tube to squeeze into before dematerializing."

The doctor's eyebrows rode up and down as he spoke, like a wind full of oakboughs. "Good idea, eh? But what did the retort retort? *Fech!* B Sirius, doctor, you'll be off on that track for months. Think of the havoc if you leave Annie to her own devices. Good point, I said—no sooner said than undone."

And Doctor Analarge flipped his cigar butt into the litter of broken glass. A tongue of white flame snapped up the milky puddle and the green fog above it, shot upwards, drilled the ceiling and roof tiles and disappeared in the evening sky.

Only a starry little sprinkle of dry glass remained. "Get it out of here, Shamp," said the doctor, waving a fresh cigar in its direction. "She's not coming, that's obvious…"

I bent over the splinters with my back to the doctor. To my chagrin, the fat nose of the fire extinguisher slid down and hung out of my collar.

"No, put away that broom and come talk with me a while. Yanneleh, save for your loyal attendance on my failures, which do have a stellar pathos of a kind, there is no reproof of my enduring self-indulgence which hath sound, or maketh a man to weep." He wept, and the room sang with the drawing of his cigar like to a plague of locusts. I swept on unsteadily, little jerks with the broom; meanwhile the extinguisher popped stubbornly out of my shirtfront.

Then he saw the thing. "*A verschlepteh krank!* A stand-in daughter with tits full of CO2, that's what I get for holing up a Personality." He pulled the French tablecloth over his knees and trembled in the fringes like an old man. "Where is she, Shamp? Get her here by sundown or my life isn't worth a nickel. I'm nothing without her."

"Steady, doctor."

"She's gone. I should be ecstatic but I'm quaking like Vesuvius." Suddenly he pulled me onto his knee. And why not? I was almost his son-in-law. All the same my tailbone protested the irregularity, shooting backwards and forwards across his well-fatted lap like a tethered frog.

"Radial *einzigmannkopfschmerz!*" said the doctor, impressed with this performance. "You're a star and a starry semaphore. I divine from those feet"—my feet, which he proposed were waving out arcane alphabets as I tried to balance—"that time has intercepted the light of my existence and punted her to my neighbor better than I.

"Well, I submit, what else can a papa do, only don't be greedy. Where is she, Shamp? Confess! confess!" The doctor jumped up and I hit the linoleum, arranged in the diphthong Œ. "Out with it!"

What to confess? "I could give you a 3-point House-Father Syndrome I worked up for a W.C.," I said from the floor, "building up to a bid for the house..."

"Perfect!" cried the doctor. "Confess, what difference does it make. What a son-in-law, already after the house. Confess, let's hear it."

I began.

How amiable are thy coney holes O lectromagnate!

For a day in thy tubes is better than a thousand in the city-solo.

I had rather be a turnstile flatfoot on the upramps of the house of Shipoff, than a star in the Barney Street theater, Big Yolk,

For the Barney Street tree star but hangs from his aspen crotch for the summer and is thrown into the garbage,

But a turnstile toady in the Depot endureth on his upramp forever and ever.

"But where is she?" said the doctor.

With the fatness of thy house I am satisfied. Yet set me up on the top rock,

For what profit is it to my blood if I go down to the Pit? Shall my dust praise thee? shall it declare—

"Never mind the Pit, go back to those coney holes, Hughbury. Details! Whose coney hole have you been in most lately? How do I get to this amiable coney hole? Out with it, pork brain. Which tube? Draw a map if necessary."

"It's only a Waste Confession, Doctor Analarge."

"Waste Confession! Confessed is confessed, how can its waste be empty? It does not conk out so fast. Did you speak? Did I hear? The heard is already conceded. Now where is my daughter!" And he kicked me in the butt.

Then I forgot myself, earnest lector.

"What do I care where your daughter is? They Court-Depoted me out of the ballgame. Either I get plugged at the Ox Roast or I hibernate till Doomsday. What's her hole beside that hole?

158

Her hole can take care of itself. All I want is a hole to hide in!"

Then I lay flat, seeing with that plain confession, that most purely Personal of topos, it was all over.

"Wait, wait," cried the doctor. He fell into his chair and his face dropped into his hands. "Where is she? You don't even know…"

I lay on my back, finished. My eyes found the spot burned through the roof by the Dog Star concoction. A little star floated in the hole, a cool and private sun of the sparest magnitude… Why had I opened my mouth? What was a kick in the *toches* beside a forty-year snore in hibernation? What were ten kicks in the buns beside a kickless bed in the grave?

The doctor snipped the end off a cigar. Illusion blown, we were now on policy.

"You don't know. *Fech!* Be that as it may, I'd like to give you a home—(*paaa, paaa*)—I will keep you a home so long as you—(*paaa, paaa*)—cultivate the Inexpressible. Now as for my daughter's hand, well, what can I say except—(*paaa, paaa*)—

> *Whatsoever woman wileth*
> *that she fulfileth*
> *howsoever men nileth.*

"*Gait, gait*, Hughby. Of life the time is a point, right? The Borigard mess will blow over, nobody will remember in three months, four. Hughbury—have you thought of hibernating for a season? Say, three months to start? Six at the limit?"

I said nothing.

"You're not planning to lie on my laboratory floor for the duration? *Gait!* what are you holding out for? An asteroid intervention?"

"You'd like to give me a home…"

"Keep you a home, keep, keep. First hibernate.

"You said I was a star—"

"*Fech!* and a neighbor better than I. Didn't it sound a bit too much like something I'd say? To my son-in-law, in a black year…" He went to the facial-surgical chair, slumped over the flushing spittoon and, sticking his finger down his throat, gave up his dinner in three installments.

"You could have been my son, pork brain. But you crossed me up, yes you did, no, not the little kissies and facies that comprise my Personality but my lab for the Inexpressible you came here and said bad words in, tracked up my floor with a ten-toed Personality. And what a Personality at that! Miserable! revolting! Therefore hibernate."

The doctor seized the two banks of hair along his part and yanked. "She left! With her belly out to here she left, you couldn't keep her. And what am I that she should stay with me? A fat old bughead. And so what. This is a doctor's laboratory, not the Ritz. This is no clubroom for her piggy boyfriends. And so hibernate or get shot, little pork, but in your pants I would certainly hibernate." The doctor leaned over me and rolled back my eyelids, his cigar stuck between his teeth. "Yellow. You know I could almost smell her on you…"

Her smell—a capsule of sal ammoniac nicked at the core of the rose, the rose of the rosefields of imperial Ghazipur. By St. Cornwallis! If I lost I lost. But surely there was a snort of that perfume yet on my unwashed collar points. I sat up.

"She was gallant."

"Aiiii! my benefactress," he said.

"A sorceress."

"Such a bitch though."

"But strong."

"A mensch! yes! A regina, a highpowered lady, mean as a snake." He fished a pen and a frayed Western Union pad out of a drawer and tossed them to me. "Take a wire—

NOW ANNIE INGRATITUDE BEING A COMPLAINT HARD TO PINPOINT SUBSTATUTORY NO FELONY PRONE TO EXAGGERATE SORE TO FIND WITH YOUR INGRATITUDE I WILL NOT TAKE ISSUE I WISH YOU VERY WELL

(Here the doctor drew a breath.)

160

AND NOW AS I DRAW TO A CLOSE I REFLECT ONCE
MORE ON THIS TOPOS INGRATITUDE AND FIND IT BE-
SIDE THE POINT INVOCATIONS OF GRATITUDE THEN IN
NO WAY OBSCURING THE ISSUE I RESORT TO THAT
WHICH I TRUST YOU WILL NOT NEGLECT GELT REPEAT
GELT MAZUMA MONEY WHAT IS THE LEAST YOU WILL
TAKE TO COME HOME TO PAPA FOR WHOLE WEEK
WEEKDAYS EVES WEEKENDS ANY ARRANGEMENT ALSO
WILL YOU CONSENT TO DISCREET CHAPERONAGE
WHEN ON THE FLY IF NOT BY ME PERSONALLY PLEASE
TO REPLY AT ONCE COLLECT WITH FIGURES LOVE PAPA
ANALARGE

"About that chaperonage," I said.

"You're a good boy," cried the doctor. "Hired!"

"Address?"

"I don't know! I don't know! Find her for me! No, stick it in a
hair oil bottle and throw it in the Sump. Why should she leave
me? I was the best father in the world, the most wise, generous
and loving..."

"Her breasts—"

The doctor smacked me in the eye. "What do you take me
for! Even a daughter's tits aren't private with a Personality.
The likes of you! *Fech!* go hibernate! go get shot. I don't care,
just quit my sight." He padded around the loft with his back to
me, pinching back a pea vine, propping a syngonium.

"I won't go. Keep me as your secretary, just till after the Ox
Roast..."

"Won't go! As my secretary! Listen closely, little pork. I've
been taking on secretaries for thirty years, I have had 314
secretaries. I am an employer in the grand tradition, the boss
become boss of his own grandboss. Those secretaries came all
in joy! And they all went, crying with relief, in three weeks at
the outside. Three hundred and fourteen down—"

"Make it 315!"

"I already counted you, porkpie. Three hundred and fourteen assistants in 30 years, of which you were, lamentably, one. But only one in 30 years ever stuck at the exit and that was yourself, bub. A suffering servant complex! Of Personalities you must be the beginning and the end, a secondary sexual character impregnated miraculously through the cringing sphincter of postick fruitlessness with a Personality consisting of You name it! up the ass! absolutely anything that crosses your path, even me! *Fech!* And all the same, regardless of what goes up it an asshole is still an asshole, porkpie, nor can an asshole be empty but requires a plug even when the proprietor has cut his last and in peace departed. So go hibernate!"

"I won't go to the Pit!"

"What! Then don't, just stay here, I'll get the lectromagnate, he'll have your butt all right."

And he slid down the pole and went out, snapping off the loft lights as he passed.

XXII
The White Bullock

I lay in the dark loft on the linoleum. The last blue cloud of cigar smoke drained away upward and there was the little star again in the ceiling hole—no, it was another one, even smaller than the last, shining with an even chillier self-possession, like the flown eyelight of some starcrossed Cornwallis gone respectably to his beheading, his little fame behind him, or rather head and head with him, divided from his little fate only by the slender nicety of the butcher's blade.

In an inexpressible humor I waited on my back for the doctor to come back with Shipoff. But no one came. A June beetle crashed mechanically time after time into the racks of clean test tubes along the wall, and the glinting lyre of laboratory glass played back mechanically. I remembered the test tube of astrodisiac Tapsvine had stuck over my ear after my 21-point Waste Confession, and felt through my pockets for it. Granted that of life the time is a point, it's a point, at times, murderously sharp for the butt that is stuck on it. There, when all measures fail, a goofer is in order.

An hour went by. All at once I realized what the doctor must have planned—that, scared to death of the lectromagnate, I would screw right out the door behind him. Just then a powerful draft sifted my ear whiskers. I rolled over and looked down. In a wall hanging loose from the Dog Star blast, intent on my escape, the doctor had left the vestibule door wide open. In fact, the whole building was swaying in the wind, and what was more, just inside it on the laboratory counter a roll of green dollar bills skittered with each gust. A kindly man the doctor! He had not only thought, he had hoped and provided that I would run. Through that door, jumping from can to can across the Depot dump, to the West Poolesville Truckers' PURE & Oasis, the highway, and freedom. But where is the next dump for a lone stray weaned on Big Yolk garbage? Where is garbage like the garbage of the city-solo? He is faithful, the stray. He might sniff up the pantslegs of his master's enemies, run blindly around and show up again where they had turned him out abruptly, but he is no wind-up mutt with a reverse button on his collar.

I slid down the pole, took the cash, and went to look for the lectromagnate.

He had set up a fair weather tent for himself in the stubblefield south towards Bosky Point on the Sumpsky Prospect, at the foot of a little hillock studded with dandelions and bottle tops. Alone and dead sober, he was trying on one silk notable's toga after another, as befitted a lectromagnate due at an Ox Roast, in front of a wardrobe mirror. The most striking piece in his outfit, however, was a vest so padded that it brought his shoulders up to a line well over his eyebrows, so that no gunshot could enter his brain, assuming he had one, without first ploughing through four or five inches of miscellaneous construction materials. He could hardly move, and no matter which toga he struggled into, he still resembled a water tower on a country railroad siding, with its two skinny poles at the bottom and a spurt of yellow birdsnests on top.

I laughed.

"The chrust! Shamp…"

He lurched around to yank down the tent flap between us, but lost his footing and sailed through the hole in the direction of his arm. In those pads there was no use kicking him. I set him upright and stuck my fistful of greenbacks under his nose.

And now I saw. His eye had a rising price in it. As for its color, the half-baked oxblood that had disappointed me in Bulimy had made progress—it ran fresh red. And floating in the whites I saw Shamp, a white bullock, now as charming in twin piles of bones and gore as he had been fair on the hoof back in Bulimy—a beast of burden at the West Poolesville Depot, in Big Yolk a voluptuary murder.

Fancy! For the first time I could make head, tail, lungs and liver of the special powers of the lectromagnate, which lay neither in brains nor charms but rather in the range of that infinitely tractile organ, Shipoff's pleasure. In every turn of luck from so-so to bad to worse (except his own of course) he found a point to dote on and play with and curl up in, thence to divide himself happily into his victim. For example, if my rise toward a lit-up lectern was his pleasure, for a while, my fall from the lectern was unrelieved rapture... It all had a wild simplicity, my fall, a one-way recoil ending in that spacious quantity, zero.

Just before zero was my hand, full of dollar bills. I began: "Where do you buy those vests, chum?"

"Sold out! store model!"

My eye picked out a glossy mugshot of Shamp in lector's threads, sticking out of Shipoff's kidney padding. I snatched. So the lectromagnate was canning up a little press release for the benefit of my retirement—

$$\text{ATTENTION}: \quad \begin{array}{l} \text{Obituary} \\ \text{Sports Page} \\ \text{Financial News} \\ \text{Around Big Yolk} \end{array}$$

Little Athens (June 24): In a convocation of solemn praise,

Sergei Shipoff's Topical Tropists, Inc., of the West Pooles-

ville Depot, today $\begin{Bmatrix} \text{commemorates} \\ \text{celebrates} \end{Bmatrix}$ the $\begin{Bmatrix} \text{posthumous} \\ \text{in absentia} \end{Bmatrix}$ grant to Hughbury Shamp, one of the original Depot lectors, of

the Annual Arslevering Polity Prize of $ .... The

$\begin{Bmatrix} \text{battered victim} \\ \text{happy winner} \end{Bmatrix}$ of the Midsummer's Day Ox Roast

speakers' marathon has been $\begin{Bmatrix} \text{interred in} \\ \text{enshrined in} \end{Bmatrix}$ Indefinite

Hibernation, $\begin{Bmatrix} \text{a funereal euphemism} \\ \text{the Honors research project} \end{Bmatrix}$ at the Depot,

according to tripodial council chairman Sergei Shipoff, also

ex officio $\begin{Bmatrix} \text{executor} \\ \text{trustee} \end{Bmatrix}$ of the $\begin{Bmatrix} \text{departed} \\ \text{victorious} \end{Bmatrix}$ lector's $\begin{Bmatrix} \text{estate.} \\ \text{award.} \end{Bmatrix}$

"The money," Shipoff told newsmen

I crumpled up the paper and bounced it off his double-crossing forehead.

And that little sortie in my own animal interest brought Shipoff also to action. In defense of my tomb, he first struggled to a sitting position.

"Boys!"

(And he blew into a stooge whistle stitched into the wrist of his padding.)

Two new novice lectors, the size of ex-ballroom bouncers, came trotting out of the hackberry brake and picked me up by the elbows.

"Thank you, boys. Starboy, for you the star is over. Why push it? Now take the rap like a Tropist—either scratch your entry and go down the hole and snore, or study the topos, go up to the Ox Roast lectern and die."

"What if I win at the Ox Roast and live? *The happy winner of the Ox Roast speakers' marathon has been enshrined in Indefinite Hibernation...*"

He waved his hand. "I don't want to see him for the next ten hours."

The bouncers led me down the upramp to the same pay toilet that Doctor Analarge had been locked up in, and bolted the door behind them.

Ten hours left.

I looked the place over.

The toilet was long gone. There was a hole to piss and crap in, and a ten-inch layer of surplus potholders strewn over the cold concrete, thanks to recent prosperous Yules in the Depot bughouse.

I thought of the Pit and those deal tables full of macaroni and potholder loops...

All reflection ended. I would never hibernate again in this world down the same hole with AUNTY.

All measures had failed. I fished for Tapsvine's dope.

Let the Ox Roast!

I held my nose and poured it down.

XXIII
The Rank Bosk Map

In my dream I blew Brakeknot up to catasteroid particles, not a bad end as ends end, except that I miss the old man, how I miss him!

It was spring on the Little Sump, Captain Shamp was young and the crew pulled strong behind him. How fine and dry she blew that March! The foredeck of the *Mercy McPhorear* was polished so bright between rains that the navigator, Mr. Peltman, much afflicted in his spine from a trouble picked up in his youth in the Bosky Point brothels and always aggravated by the river air, could do his celestial computations a full two weeks without being tipped aft in his deck chair, by studying the stars upside down in the deck varnish...

Splendid days! I lived without reflection. But in time, as the choke cherry groves that lined Front and River streets all up and down the levee country gave up their petals to the stream, after a long dream of glassy water and quiet patrols, the summer sun began to drum the blood in my temples, and I thought once more of cracking old Brakeknot's neck.

I had put my ambition away from me all winter, knowing too well that the vow to undo Sergeant Brakeknot sprang not from love of duty, nor fealty to my masters, nor zeal for the fatherland, nor yet for love of my own life, but rather from the appetite for revenge merely, personal revenge, private, solo, singular and homecooked revenge and revenge only.

And yet, as I was a man little inclined to words, few were the nights that winter when I did not rise with the late bell like one in a fever, and drawing on my boots, climb to the fo'c'sle, where pacing in solitude and silence but for the flap of the Sump against the bulkhead, I wrestled with the devil of my rage in the starlight. And when I cried for succour this came out of my mouth instead—

Eli, Eli! *The roving corpse of Brakeknot eats up my lungs & liver, and the thought of Brakeknot's triumph wrings the blood from my heart. O Eli! watch me! I'll rend his ass to shoestrings before the summer is out!*

Thus I resolved to deliver myself of this violent and enervating passion on schedule, though it cost me immortal life! I swore that by midyear, when the beanstalks bent, I would blast the old Sergeant to the bosom of his causes.

As I take no pleasure in carnage, and the river had been peaceful since Groundhog Day, I determined to spare the innocent in his command as I trusted he would, as a gentleman, spare mine.

On Midsummer's Eve I took two days' leave of my crew on personal excuses and rode overland to Bosky Point at the mouth of the Sump, where "The Rank Bosk Map" rode in harbor. I soon had assurance that, as foreseen, the Sergeant had proclaimed a general leave on his vessel, as is the custom in the levees on the eve of Midsummer.

I discovered, moreover, that by luck, prescient of the onset after dinner of one of the seizures of nocturnal rage, without cause, which had troubled his later years, and for the space of which, at sea, he allowed that his crew batten him down securely in the coal hold, Sergeant Brakeknot had instead this afternoon dismissed all hands and even the night watch, that for once he might rage at liberty on "The Rank Bosk Map," in peace and privacy as of old.

Captain to captain, we would see bold contest.

I go aboard in stealth. I have charges and fuses in plenty and I set to it with dispatch and an easy mind, for a man who raves like old Brakeknot will never overtake me unawares. And indeed the Sergeant can be heard already, raving in the ward-room and the afterdeck, lo, he raves on the bridge and in the fo'c'sle and below in the captain's dining room, and in the chartroom and the barrel holds from his raving is not still. I pay no heed to his words until I have wreathed "The Rank Bosk Map" in flowers of saltpetre, gartered her in fuses and pow-dered her with powder from her flagmast to her keel. She is wired to blow in one-and-twenty minutes.

Even as I set the last charge I hear, bellowed out from amidships, my own name, then nothing!

I am vexed. It has been my design to track down the raving to the body, then subdue and finish Brakeknot in fair combat hand to hand—my youth and foresight pitted against his age, hindsight, and the power of that maniac rage.

As for "The Rank Bosk Map"—after I win, the blast serves to scour away the ignominy of the corpse, to let the Old Dog go up and down with his ship, and to thwart the homicide squad and the Bosky Point papers.

Now with no raving to follow, I cannot find Brakeknot at all. I race about amidships from quarter to quarter. At last a saw-ing noise, conceivably human breath, directs me to the ward-room, where I find a great wheel of blackbread leaning rak-ishly on its edge against the sideboard, a wedge the size of a man's head hacked out of it. The smell of cheap spirits is strongly about and a sticky ring from a now absent jug is edged in crumbs on the countertop…

I climb the coiled stairway to an open hatch. It is Brakeknot! He is leaning backwards over the deck railing at the foot of the flagmast, hanging straight out over the water most perilously, almost perpendicular, a corn liquor jug dangling overboard from the fingers of one hand, and the great lump of bread hanging down, stuck onto the fingers of the other.

He is snoring.

I clapped my hand to my head. "Brakeknot! What have you gone and done!" The Sergeant cracked an eye and said: "I'll be blowed, Captain! Don't ask me! Is this your ship or mine?" I held out my arms to the old stiff, unable to speak. Then he knew me. "My own boy!" He reversed the angle of his spine so suddenly that the bread and whiskey at the ends of his arms swung forward, crashed and wound around each other, while his chin bobbed down to his boot tops. When he tried to straighten the victuals flew back again over the rails and his face fell back in a flap, so that he cried upwards, straight at the moon:

"Now it does the old dog's heart good to see you, Hughby my boy! Here's my hand, but to be truthful I can't take a step, my dogs are stuck in this block under the flag pull and a mercy it is, or I'd be down there again with them goddamned embroaderies not fit to wipe your butt-end with..."

I ran to the balustrade—the flags of Bulimy County and "The Rank Bosk Map" wriggled darkly in the dark water where he'd dropped them.

I consulted my papa's old railroad watch. What bum luck! Ten minutes to drag the old fudd home. The Sergeant was snoring again, the point of his nose straight up in the wind, his mouth sagging like a carpetbag. *"Rachacheh-e-e-e-e!"* A little scarf of spittle tacked over his cheek and blew south on the river wind.

Hang it all, I loved him. The dream turned around, and suddenly I saw the Bulimy County paradegrounds, the treacherous bleachers without seats or railings, the girls from the high school typing class in pink and blue suits with chalky white linen pumps on their feet, the powdery rubber balloons, the town dogs adrift in packs, lifting their legs one by one to piss on the shiny black curtain of the beer booth, sprinkling the besotted citizens' Sunday pantscuffs. Finally I saw the Optimist Glee Club march on the dilapidated bleachers in a body, hanging onto the corners of their music books in the wind, while, scaling the sea of them, slowly, with dignity, from one end of the grandstand to the other, came the "Bull Lily Champ." In the arms of Brakeknot the Bulimy County red longhorn chewed benignly and eternally on a green silk ground, bouquets of white lilies spraying out of both sides of its mouth and waving as the flag waved in the mild June blow.

> *Where never-ceasing pleasures roll*
> *And praises never die.*
>
> *I am bound...*

Earnest lector, it was back at the Bulimy County Optimist Society's Annual Sing that I made this small revision. For if Providence is hindsight, mastery is hindsight threaded blindly into the future, a ribbon brainless as a worm drawn through the eyehole of repetitious sufferings and thrown like a mooring in the general direction of the next station. Mastery is Providence, if you're lucky.

As for me I found my little dog track all right, a track prior to all the masters' tropos winding deliriously up that dusty hill of grass between the graveyard and the parade ground, into the rank bushes over the railroad yards.

The first thing I saw was Brakeknot, the Sergeant-at-Arms fresh, if fresh is the word, from his yearly foray into numberless green tomato pies and fried chicken halves, and oceanic lavages of 2.0 beer, plus a nip or two or twelve with the president, secretary and vice president under the bleachers—a solitudinous old gentleman and a bachelor, fond of jokes, of good appetite when well fed, fond on days like today of the ladies, on other days jarred by their frontal approach to matters close to his heart—just now though smiling freely at his benefactresses as he poles himself up the bleachers with a flagpole in each hand.

On top at last, he oscillates back and forth up there on the far western point of the bandstand, back and forth, moving not with the music nor with any singly earthly thing, but with all things, moving back and forth in the divine submissiveness of an advanced drunk, moving with all things, helpless not to move, in fact dancing, brainless as a tree...

"You fell off?"

"Yep—backwards." He was smiling again from the flag pulley block.

"Not the sweet soloist from the south grange who sang himself to mortal expiration...?

"Hah! hah! *racheheh-e-e-e-hah*!" This was so funny that the blackbread finally slipped from his fingers and splatted into the river below. He held onto the liquor jug, however.

"A post office clerk in real life, I suppose," I said bitterly.

"No but warm! A rate and ticket clerk on the Bulimy Court-House & East Gopher Landing Line, if you wish to know the truth."

"Your little fame?"

"Everybody knows the ticket seller..."

Not even a conductor with his rote strings of topos—*West Bulimy, Bulimy, Bulimy Court-House—all aboard*. We were silent, melancholy over his bygone fibs. A ticket seller on a 12-mile line—one old wood-burning diamond stacker, with an ex-chicken coop for a roundhouse...

"All the same," said the Sergeant defensively, after a while, "that old bullgine could roll it up in twenty-one minutes..."

Twenty-one minutes!

"Sergeant Brakeknot! We'll have to go overboard! I wired 'The Rank Bosk Map' with TNT—she's going to blow any second!"

"Can't! Stuck!—you go."

I ran over to the Sergeant, locked my arms around his waist, lodged my head in his hollow armpit and pried. There was nothing to the old coot but gooseflesh, cross-ties and whiskers, but he was dead stuck. "Wired 'The Rank Bask Map'!" he said, throwing his arm around my neck as I pushed and holding me hard against him. "Why my own boy! Hughbury Shamp, you natural born—"

Constellation
"The Rank Bosk Map"

Snow, snow, it's snowing Brakeknot. Who would have thought that a six-pint stiff like Brakeknot could snow for hours, softly, quietly, whisker by whisker?

XXIV
The Ox Roast

Before I had come to my senses, they registered all the same, in strangled gasps like a Tennessee camp meeting harmonium,

—The pay toilet door wheeling open (it was not quite dawn).

—Meaty forearms yanking me out to the Sumpsky Prospect. A crawl in the fog—Shipoff's two bouncer-lectors half rolled, half carried me down to West Poolesville Landing.

—Then over the West Poolesville Bridge on all fours. This part I remember! In the space at the bottom of the guard-rails was the freshness of starlight floating in the Sump, the breathless empire renewed for love of the sprinkled soul of Brakeknot...

—An oldfashioned white taxicab, its leaky cavity sucking wind, Shipoff perched on the pegseat, black silk Ox Roast toga hissing around his knees like a turkish bath.

—And in the moonlight the cut-up whip of the highway lane marker snapping at the windshield, the liquid chime of breaking glass, somebody, Shipoff no doubt, throwing out one two-ounce snort bottle after the other.

All at once it was full day. Ground sparrows twittered in the honeysuckle. My socks drooped over my sandals, soaked with dew.

We stood in a field north of the city-solo, at the start of an east bank detour devised by the lectromagnate to bypass subterranean saboteurs. The taxi putt-putted away in a thread of mist. Then Shipoff started walking, his two bulls dragging me along toward a tumbledown subway upramp overgrown with blackberry bushes and burrs.

Down, down, the sunny field behind us, for a long time nothing but breath and the dull chock of feet against mossy rails. Shipoff stopped to listen. I leaned against the wall. The fog rolled around my brain one last time and departed. And then I heard the faraway, thick-lipped growl on top of us, swelling and shrinking uneasily. A little farther and we entered the yellow vault of a Big Yolk subway station.

"The Sump is really roaring," I said, in a sweat.

"You mean the Ox Roast is!" Shipoff looked at me. His heavies were strapping him into the padded vest. *Poing!* a shell bounced off the hatch cover.

All at once, now more than ever it seemed rich to hibernate, if one could just get around the Pit with its three homicidal lady volunteers and its tables full of beanbags and elbow macaroni. All tubes led to Big Yolk, but if a body hooked north in time instead of surfacing at the city-solo, at the other end of that tunnel he found a field loud with grasshoppers, where an unemployed lector could snore in the grass on Midsummer's Day, even though five miles downtube as the snake crawls, all of Big Yolk blew itself away in a free-for-all.

Shipoff was trying on wigs in the gum machine mirror, grunting in his vest. I said: "I think I'll hibernate after all."

"Well you might, if you live, Hughby."

"But that's my final choice."

"I'll make a note of it."

"S-H-I-P-O-F-Fffff, Shipoff to the lectors' breakfast table." The voice of the crier boomed out of the tubes to the south. The World-Friar followed it out of the blackness with a laugh. He wore a false nose. Waxed and blueblackened mustachios hung down to his Ox Roast butler's toga.

"Fancy you showing," said Shipoff. "What are they saying, the buzzards?"

"Everything, everything!" cried the World-Friar. "It restores your faith in the primitive lector in every mother's son and father's daughter... Need a boost?"

We looked up at the hatch, which rattled under a hailstorm of unfriendly objects.

"Seven-thirty, let's go," said the World-Friar, tossing away his cigarette and taking his post by the hatch. Earnest lector, I saw it in his eye: it was kicks! By St. Cornwallis, he was dying for one of us to get it.

I wondered if I'd meet Sergeant Brakeknot in the other world, or if, knowing our mutual tastes, we might not both make it back to this one. O drat! How had we forgotten to pick some midway point—like the Midway Big Dipper at the Bosky Point Speedway Midway—Midsummer's Eve midnight, in the year 2000...

"—Two, three, SHOOT!" The four of us heaved Shipoff up through the hatch, a strawberry blond wiglet bouncing a little at the top of his vest, tied on by two strings.

Above us the shooting did not really increase but rather swung orchestrally, as they picked out the lectromagnate under his wig, toward the hornbeam groves to the south where the speakers' table was laid. All at once the basso swells were pierced at that end by Shipoff's voice, shrill with terror, pouring the syllables of my name into a microphone. By the time the roar peaked around the lectern, the lectromagnate was back pounding the door over my head. His two tough guys loomed at my shoulders—I raised the hatch.

With a pneumatic sigh, he drifted down to the floor tiles. He had lost the wig, and the remains of the black celebrity's toga hung from his shoulders in flickering tongues—out of the vest the padding erupted in spurts, but he was alive and crawling and had managed to grab a gold-threaded white lector's toga for me as he ran, as well as a gold foil laurel wreath, the same item Tapsvine had suggested I steal for my 21st W.C. point.

"You're on, starboy."

His boys stripped me down and rolled me up in the toga.

177

But the lectromagnate himself clapped the glittering leaves to my forehead.

They pricked.

"Thanks for the point," I said.

"My pleasure." And he patted the thatch of hair that stuck out of it. "Think, the lectern of Big Yolk lecterns—a flown-up lector at last."

"I'd rather hibernate..."

Shipoff snapped his fingers and the two lector-heavies started closing on me. Suddenly out of a pleat in his butler's toga the World-Friar pulled a blue hypodermic, a huge dose, a horse syringe.

"Thanks but no thanks," I cried, backing away.

The four gentlemen tightened their circle.

So that was the tropos expected! To go to my only lectern not on my feet but on my knees, to enter the hornbeam grove doped senseless and in swaddling clothes, painlessly leaking my lifesblood from twenty holes, like a cherub in a piazza...

I jumped through the hatch, popping the lid back in the grass, and stood on it in a rage.

"Okay, so I was born on the first of last week!" I shouted.

Shipoff's whisper floated up to me out of the hole: "Jawbones, Hughby, close that thing..."

"Say, that's a hiss of a different crawler. No shot, lectromagnate. I want you to hear this. *Madame Arslevering! Masters, lectors, terrorists, guests!* This is Hughbury Shamp, up from the Depot pay phone, cutting the cord. In the name of St. Cornwallis,

"Goodbye to the Topical Tropists!

"Hello to his O! so reluctant demise with selected

XXV

Hindthoughts On His Own Magnificence

"They said I was a star, and like a good lector I fell for it—

The lector is cheerful!
All luck he commends!
The lector believes
He is loved by his friends!

"—And yet in the backparts or lower side of my magnificence are certain points of interest: now he who would not look me in the bunghole"—(I pulled my toga up and showed Shipoff my ass)—"let him please himself."

("Sssst—the hatch, Hughby!")

They laughed! I looked up. It was a tremendous Ox Roast whose laughter rippled over the Arslevering big top in breakers and wavelets, laughing faces in a grassy sea—a huge crowd densest in the whitewashed porticos at the top, thinning but still packed along the bog banks, spilling over onto the footbridges...

The stench of singed ox hair tweaked my nostrils.

I laughed. "Well! All here I see. And here I am likewise, the star himself, under fire it is true from hostile constituents, yea even from the old starpicker Shipoff himself! In fact here is the star dangling by his own middle finger"—(I showed Shipoff the finger)—"from his twinkling parameres, my finest points

---

179

crumbling like roquefort cheese under my fingernails, while somehow the *star* blazes away, always the same, the *star*, unperturbed by my imminent departure.

"If this be gloria mundi, friends, where is the blood so cold it would come between the star and his nostalgia? The star is excusable…he may fart 20 minutes on the plumbing of his causes." And I blew a fine fart down the hole in the lectromagnate's direction.

("Hughby old starboy! Please! The hatch!") I looked down. At the first rain of arrows his bodyguard was cheesing it down the tubes. Shipoff lay on his back, floundering in his padding on the floortiles.

Below they laughed! They clapped! Vasselina Arslevering waved from the pueblo widow's walk, stomping and tweeting through her front teeth. I watched the lectromagnate roll slowly toward the Poolesville tube but the ones that wanted him were already at the edge and dropping over…

And I, I was in the spirit. The spirit was on me, I was lost in the spirit.

"Now a topos for Weatherall Brakeknot—a little fame at the last upramp. For **Prior to Every Lector** is that solitudinous old gentleman, the bachelor wasting in his boarding house, who experiences magnificence in absentia, in extenso, who striking the waters of Meribah out of a schnapps bottle, floats his lost progeny to stars. If not fame he has—what?—friends among famous ghosts after all, a real comrade in spite of his luckless submersion at points of acute Providential intersection…

"He is off on his last go-round, friends, pottering along the boardwalk at Bosky Point. Now what is this urge, with his railroad pension in his pocket, with the terminal in sight, after the last ticket is sold and the long song and dance of proscribed labors is done, to poke in the garbage cans along the sea edge— to leave the Sunday paper, the corpse of last week, on a parkbench, and plumb the crust of cigar butts and hotdog ends, into the Chrustmas pie of the unknown?

"He feeds the pigeons…

"On holidays he lights little fires in the trashcans and runs!

"What is left to the Son of Brakeknot, after the pigeons are fed, having his old dog track by rote before the last Starstream Special tools out of his roundhouse, but humble silence, his head beam snuffed out at the first twinkle?

I had time out of mind given it up as a lost
cause, given myself over, I mean, a pre-
destined lector, though without a drop of
true lector *blood in my veins …*

"Miles at sea, fans! on the contrary! It is a man's duty to let himself off…

"So I say *Shamp! you have Shamp's opinion in this matter. And what is Shamp's yea or nay? Who would go to sea in an opinion when the waves are never the same twice? Do you require to be praised by a man who kicks himself every quarter hour? Would you try to please a Shamp whose solo for a year, whose whole song and dance, was the tropos* please and thank you?

"Old boardwalk arsonist, the sea shines through at last. For what could be the topos of Shamp run aground in the city-solo but always the same haggard potboy, his face an aerial view of metropolitan Big Yolk, his smile a crenellated skyline, his track a ticker tape spurted out across the major intersections, his nozzle enacting a public shower of words above the lectern, while behind the lectern his moons rest sore disposed, the backparts or lower side of his magnificence shuddering unrepealed behind the drapery.

"An asshole like the other assholes! Assholes all.

"What? It is not sufficient for the Son of Brakeknot? But surely that man were greedy of space who should desire to fly when all the world were at a crawl…

"But neither should he hang around the subway exit, neither coming nor going, his eyehole raw from the brine of repetitious sufferings, his butt-end itched to death by his ingrown follicle of Preeminence…

"Lest he be the crumpled map in the glove compartment of

—

181

his experience, let him shed once a year! let him shuck his dead skin for the fire, and burn 'The Rank Bosk Map' whereon played all his experience.

"Burn for old Brakeknot!

"For Midsummer's Day, BURN!"

I wound out of my Ox Roast lector's toga, borrowed a match, poured a brandy over it and set it aflame. Cheers! Laughter! Suddenly all over the Arslevering tuft hundreds of little fires broke out in the grass, as thousands of Ox Roasters pulled off their togas in a pandemonium of relief, red togas ablaze for the Œkists, green for Re-natured Greenards, blue for Chrustians and plainclothes coppers, white and gold for Tropists and unaffiliated lectors—indigo, burnt umber, hyacinth, pearl...

The filmy togas were consumed in a flash. The naked guests stopped for a moment and stared at each other. Then with a howl they fell on the lawn furniture, cracked it to pieces and set it afire. The quartermile of white clapboard summerhouse, the balustraded kiosks fell swiftly to sticks and to flames. Now bare asses flocked to the bandstand. Each instrument was handed down and torched, solo, lovingly, alight—violin strings popped delicately, one by one, at the fringe of the conflagration, while at its heart the burning piano ragged with violent delight.

Ever starward the black smoke spiralled, an offertory perfume for the twinkling nostril of my friend.

Far below I saw Michael McCorkle dragging the body of Shipoff toward a footbridge—the lectromagnate of Big Yolk and the Americas plucked out of unseasonable hibernation, leaves in his hair. I saw that his left eye was rolled out of sight and his right eye glorified forever and ever—fixed eternally in "voluntary" oculomotor imbalance #3, with which he must have tried, in vain, to freeze his attackers at the last moment.

Even so I composed my mind, opened my mouth and shouted after him:

"Ringmaster Shipoff! may the rats bear you away in chops! may the unmarked bones of the lectromagnate gleam in Big Yolk tenement house stairwells, even unto the Second Going!"

And I started for the subway. Then remembering that Shipoff's bodyguard had run up the northern tubes, I made for a tube ramp on the southern side. On my way I passed Vasselina Arslevering tightrope-walking stark naked on the main pueblo roof clothesline, firing the kerosene-soaked porticos all around her to a grinning crescent of flame.

I stopped to watch. As I did she caught sight of me and with love in her one good eye, leaped twenty feet into the crowd.

I bolted to the south upramp, and crouched in the first pay phone down the tube to watch her fly past. No sooner had she disappeared than the World-Friar Tapsvine swung over the entrance rail gaucho-style and loped towards the lightless tunnel.

Fraulein Analarge followed close behind him, in spite of her swollen belly. "Take me!"

He stopped suddenly and with a tolerant smile stepped back towards her along the track platform. He pulled out a roll of twenties, split it in half, and gave her one.

"High time you gave me something, daddy-O."

He turned again to go.

"Take me!"

So it was Tapsvine's baby that had set Doctor Analarge raving on my tail. As for the inexpressibly uncharacteristic request on the part of daughter Annie—*Take me*—even a revolting nature like hers never loved to part with the heart that betrayed it. Such was the love for the World-Friar that bloomed under the crust of the celebrated bitch Analarge. There was also, to be sure, a small matter of 21 counts of felonious fraud coming up in the Court of Big Yolk in August to speed this amorous adventure.

"Take me!" But he was already in the tunnel. "I'd like to have your balls in a jar," she called after him, maybe thinking of the units of the World-Friar's Museum.

183

He came back for a moment: his tiny insensible eyes glittered up from the tube mouth, as soulless as stars. *Take me,* I thought—but I clung to the empty phonebooth and it passed.

At Sundown I reached the Depot and, seeing a fiery light from the upramp, ran down the Sumpsky Prospect toward the doctor's laboratory. The walls were down. The gothic vestibule was entirely dismantled; its fluted sheets lay in a heap at the foot of the aspens. Only the door to the laboratory hung by the wall studs, banging in the wind.

I went in. At the loft hole the rope ladder was pulled up and hooked to one side.

What I had seen from the subway upramp was not fire but a great white light shining out of the upper story, a light so bright and sheer I couldn't look into it. And when I backed away from the empty laboratory I saw the doctor walk out of the middle of this star with an exalted countenance and a telescope at his eye, pointed, as he had somehow pointed the vast, powdery, sifting beams, toward the southern sky, "The Rank Bosk Map," and Sirius newly rising.

Dog Days & Harvest Home

They carted the doctor away again for that one, with extra celerity when he explained to the lieutenant of the West Poolesville psycho division that he had been pulling down the lab not because he had heard the news of the Topical Tropists' downfall at the Arslevering Ox Roast, but because he was receiving premonitory messages from the Dog Star, in reply to certain recent "boudoir detonations" of his own, "in the direction of the Inexpressible."

Later they let him out again when the "conversational scintillation" he claimed to have observed in the expanded aureole of Sirius was confirmed by Big Yolk meteorologists, who traced it, however, to the great Ox Roast conflagration, as reflected over Big Yolk in the evening smog bank.

A natural mistake. A few weeks later, however, he was back in the cooler for observation, having learned that his daughter Annie, five days after being delivered of a son, had jumped the ambulance transporting her from B.Y. Lying-In prison ward back to the women's hoosegow in West Hinnstead—had successfully outrun the 6th Precinct gumshoes, probably procured a forged passport and by now had vanished into the rain forests of equatorial South America.

Thirteen months later, the World-Friar Tapsvine flew into Miami from Manaus, under contract to circumvent moralist regression at a motel chain stockholders' convention with an exorbitant ($300 a head) penitential session at the outset. He confirmed in a press conference at the time that the doctor's daughter had indeed joined him in the Orinocan jungle hinterland uninvited, that he had left her three months since in official concubinage to a 21-member Quiuian protectorate of elders which ate, slept, fought and procreated as a man, and that her return was "not expected." Whether this exhausting change of estate was her pleasure or Tapsvine's penalty remains a matter of speculation.

As for her son, the Big Yolk newspapers reported the birth on July the Fourth, ten days post Ox Roast, of "Hughbury Analarge Shamp," a name affixed to the birth certificate by the municipal registrar following a custom in motherless illegitimacies when the father is "definitely ascertained."

I did not complain.

And in fact it was not only that this Shamp came to the light of the world on my own birthday and bears my name, nor that that birthday coincides as well with one of the happier martyrdoms of St. Cornwallis, nor that the mother of the kid had once colonized my self-possession, nor that the baby's grandpop, the doctor, was once my master and helpmeet, though he threw me out in the end. Nor was it my reluctance to come to litigation, from my retirement, over certain well-placed forgeries that positively guaranteed that the new Hughby would bear my name, if uncontested, and that certain little bills and charges would pop up regularly from that day forward in my little box in the West Poolesville P.O.

Not that I didn't make the rounds of these points and follow the track of these associations around and around in their day. But what seemed natural to me as I sat here in my retirement, all alone in the tubes down the Depot upramp, my little fame behind me, at the end of my lector's career, the Tropists all flown or scattered over the city-solo—all alone in the empty Concourse, the north field, my leaf house in season—with a hole to myself and only me to go down it—here was a homeless body who needed a place to hole up, and why not...?

He comes in the summer and listens to Shamp. An earnest lector, last of the kind.

It was generally observed after the Ox Roast conflagration that the art of the lector was in its decadence, though in fact it had never had its day, not the high summer day that Shipoff previsioned for it. But a certain exhaustion settled on the profession post Ox Roast, after the exuberance of relief had spent itself, seeing how the warring factions at the Colloquium on Polity had scraped by without annihilating each other only by unanimously annihilating the entire Polis.

And in fact that was the last Arslevering Midsummer Ox Roast and Colloquium at Little Athens. For with all its vegetation consumed in the blaze, after every retaining root, bulb, corm, blade, stem, graft, and peduncle once so dearly inserted into the Arslevering tuft had boiled off to steam and carbon along with every pillar and beam of every colonnade and portico, it was scarcely a month before the famous quartermile reclaimed at such grief from the Great Morass at the city center had slid back into the muck. Vasselina Arslevering declined to rescue it, for it reminded her of the faulty McCorkle. Here she had wooed him, here she had wed him, here their marriage had been perverted by the influence of the lectromagnate Shipoff.

As for McCorkle, for some years he would be spotted in this or that European capital or winter resort by a society columnist hard up for an item. He had smuggled the remains of his philosopher-lover aboard a freighter, and spent the rest of his recorded life on a demented transcontinental pilgrimage, sowing a few putrefied particles of the lectromagnate out of a stainless steel valise at each stopping place, according to a detailed itinerary tracked out for him by the "voice" of the martyr, the Shipovian Yevlenkovich. He never returned to Vasselina.

He was not missed. Immediately after the Ox Roast conflagration the Arslevering heiress enthusiastically disencumbered the remainder of the family piecrust fortune and plunged it into a great hotel on the Sumpsky Prospect, erected on the same spot where the doctor's prefabricated laboratory had once gone up overnight. At the same time she impoverished the arts in Big Yolk for years by transferring the whole of her deductible donations to the Clean-Up-The-Sump Campaign from West Poolesville to Bosky Point.

All this she did for Shamp, earnest lector. But my hole is my refuge.

In my honor she raised this hotel that blocks my view of the lower Sump, though an occasional fish tin still protrudes, after an April downpour, from the putting green that was the Depot dump in another day.

Vasselina inhabits the penthouse. Her poured concrete window bays are molded into ornate lecterns, each topped with a soft white light. Just below, the twenty-fifth floor is likewise always lit up, always unoccupied. She holds it on standing reservation for me, and every Midsummer's Eve comes a bellboy with a card, renewing my invitation.

I burn it for old time's sake.

For in the end I have one real pleasure, and that is my joy to be quit of whatever, to have nothing but my hole and the meadow at the far end. There were masters I loved and opposed, who made their points and departed. But it's never too late to end anew, and all of those topos collapse, in time, back into the soft but steadily widening stream that bears along my name.

What is there, earnest lector, if a man be more than his topos and tropos, more than his points and tracks, his comings and goings and the stations of his mail? Is there no more to reap for the likes of Shamp, who lets it all go but the field it flows through? Nor can a field be empty but fills with his passing whistle, the breath that escapes him as he goes down the track all solo, one long whistle banding, filling, overflowing the summer sky.

On Midsummer's Day we light a bonfire in that meadow,

Shamp and Shamp the younger, in honor of Brakeknot and my lector's life which rolled away from the Ox Roast with even a little fame riding the blinds. We wander down the tracks, lose the time, sometimes coming over a green hill like the others to Bosky Point, the mouth of the Sump, the bay and the open sea.

Or we take to the field, not because the green part of nature is less puzzling to me than other parts, but because the summer which crowns it is abundant and gentle. It is enough. The roof strips of my twig house I filched from the hotel construction site down the Sumpsky Prospect. They were light—there were more than I needed—I carried them down on my back...

After the first snow I go down the hole, scratch, reflect, look in on the schnapps cellar, putter around and water my pea plants, follow the stream where it trickles, down this tube or that. Sometimes I pop up in Big Yolk and walk the gray pavements of the city-solo where Soltero's feet once clattered toward the harbor. Often I go to the chapel-loft to sit in the gutter window and, invoking St. Cornwallis, I contemplate the hotel that blocks my view.

The Hotel Shamp! Colossal, passive, maximum, iridescent, gluttonous and solo. You are my fame. I am your vacancy. You wait and wait upon my reservation. Accept my excuses! As you are my vision, I am your pore. Breathe through this hole! We were comrades once.

Hindthoughts on
Shamp of the City-Solo

*Still for Larry Eldredge, my favorite master,
and no mean miscellanist himself.
And for Bruce McPherson.*

W ith the passage of time I have become more like anyone else:
more a reader of *Shamp of the City-Solo* than the writer of it.
The creator of that mad, embarrassing, infantile, rather gorgeous
book will come again no more. But I knew her well—parts of her,
at least. People expect a writer's first novel to be the obviously
autobiographical one, but she, the old Jaimy Gordon, was too self-
allergic in her twenties to indite a recognizable self-portrait in
prose, except in a sort of cipher.

Her brain had been colonized by certain texts, not that she
thought all the writers of those texts the greatest of literary masters, but their idiosyncratic styles, hortatory habits of mind and
wide but hodge-podgy learning gave a hermit crab's portable
structure to her own soft-bodied tendencies in those directions.
Under her seashell derby she harbored Marcus Aurelius in the
Long translation and Rabelais in the Urquhart; Francis Bacon and
Thomas Browne were in there; Richard Burton's translation of the
Thousand Nights and a Night was along for the ride; she felt queerly
attached, cranially, to the by turns long-winded, by turns self-
despairing parts of Coleridge, and to the miscellanist's distract-
ibility and disorder (*like a Sott as I was*) of John Aubrey, the shape
of whose life, by the way, especially his relief at his own bank-
ruptcy, was not unlike Hughbury Shamp's. They were a tradition
into which she fit—however odd a family they looked in the
present day. Just as Shipoff, Dr. Analarge and the World-Friar
Tapsvine are her hero Hughbury Shamp's masters, these old writers were Gordon's masters, ersatz fathers in the department of

191

language, for Gordon was a willfully parentless child at that age, as Shamp was at his.

Even back then she would have admitted that the sound of her masters' prose, their extravagantly elastic periods, their irregular grammar and chewy metaphor, hospitality to vocabularies of every provenance, cracked periphrasis and asymmetrical antithesis, was her counselor as much as any of their philosophies. From Bacon and Marcus, she learned to form aphorisms as though human character could be rationally improved. Of course what is noble in Marcus is ridiculous, even hysterical, in Hughbury Shamp, and yet owing to her prose models this can only be hysteria with baroque sonorities and a classical frame. From Marcus as well she learned the harmonics of "Thanks All Around": thus her narrator Shamp opens by acknowledging every absent master for lessons learned. Some of Marcus's lessons she was not above plagiarizing direct to the lector's manuals of the city-solo: *From my brother Severus...I learned...to believe that I am loved by my friends...* comes out in Shamp's "Hindthoughts on His Own Magnificence" as

> *The lector is cheerful!*
> *His luck he commends!*
> *The lector believes*
> *He is loved by his friends!*

It's true such lessons are jokes in the Shipovian world, where Shamp's first master broadcasts his scams with every utterance. *I did him wrong,* Shipoff laments:

> *I did him wrong, the time it took would shame a lesser man,*
> *but I say, On Shipoff! courage! plough on to the next sucker.*

If it was the handsomeness of the prose that first drew her after their models, still there was something sincere in, for example, Gordon's ransacking of Marcus's Stoicism for her own fictive purposes. His serene arguments against attachment to things of this world so enchanted her that she could not help rustling them from their proper time and herding them into the present as a rhetoric of luxurious loss, a consolation of emptiness. This ubiquitous refrain from *Shamp of the City-Solo* is lifted straight from the *Meditations*:

> *For that which a man has not, how can anybody take it away*
> *from him?*

(And John Aubrey, who like the author of *Shamp of the City-Solo* could never be quite respectable, wrote:

> *Never quiet, nor anything of happiness till divested of all, 1670, 1671: at what time providence raised me (unexpectedly) good friends...with whom I was delitescent* [lying hidden].... *From 1670, to this very day (I thank God), I have enjoyed a happy concealment.*

Likewise in the end Hughbury Shamp goes down his hole to enjoy *the pleasures...of non-negotiability, home-hole, "pig-exile."*)

In those days Jaimy Gordon was sure she would never write a word of her own life into fiction, but at this distance I can see how *Shamp of the City-Solo* had roots in what you might incautiously call real life. For example, when she was writing *Shamp of the City-Solo*, Jaimy Gordon had just come from three years of work among convinced and unabashed if rinky-dinky hustlers—the half-mile racetrack circuit—so that in any gaily dog-eat-dog world she felt right at home. Yes, she was straight from the racetrack—although the racetrack is far, far from real life, is a fictitious and fantastical world if ever there was one. Then, come to think of it, at the heart of *Shamp* is an even more direct transplant from living memory, though of *a dream and folly*. Long before she had ever heard of Thomas Browne, when she was about eight years old, in the same moment she understood that she would live once and die once, and the world that had not expected her would go on without her, and the stream that had washed her up on this hump would close over her sinking away, as if she had never been—in that moment she became obsessed with fame. Or more exactly, she became convinced, at the age of eight, that life without the runaway truck ramp of fame was doom (she would be trudging in her worried way to school and she would take that word in her mouth and suck on it, *doom, doom, doom*)—that without fame to deliver it from claustrophobia, life was so small as to be practically over already. Or as Hughbury Shamp would later put it,

> *I said that without a little renown for me at the center, life would seem to me a mistake, and consciousness just as well visited on a telephone booth or a railroad tie as on me...*

But the World-Friar Tapsvine, Shamp's master of religion, says,

> *Never put your money on the lizzie which transports you, for...*

its climb is a switchback on a parlous trestle
its descent a blind speedball devoid of judgement
its coupling unsure
its mileage a dream and folly of expectation.

The World-Friar must have been reading *Hydriotaphia, or Urne Buriall* by Sir Thomas Browne, for in a corrupt sort of way he is quoting that first of the first of Jaimy Gordon's prose masters: *Diuturnity is a dream and folly of expectation.*

I think it must be allowed that when Jaimy Gordon first came across Doctor Browne, her quickening was not to *mere* words (though words can never be *mere*. They are all we have.) Although he spoke from three centuries away and from a presumption of Christian eternity that comprehended all too well the terror it was intended to stave off, his words came to her as balm for their own desolation. The antiquarian doctor has been poking through old bones and relics, and this occasions page upon page of combings through his own masters from antiquity, an inventory of the burial practices of the pagans, and finally his own knotty and elegiac ruminations:

> *It is the heaviest stone that melancholy can throw at a man to tell him he is at the end of his nature; or that there is no further state to come, unto which this seems progressionall, and otherwise made in vaine...*

He must admire the pagans their reckless courage:

> *Unto such as consider none hereafter, it must be more than death to dye, which makes us amazed at those audacities, that durst be nothing, and return unto their chaos again.*

And he considers the last resort of fame, that wild hope of mortal unbelievers like Jaimy Gordon at eight and Shamp at sixteen, even as he snatches it away:

> *Oblivion is not to be hired: The greater part must be content to be as though they had not been, to be found in the Register of God, not in the record of man.... Diuturnity is a dream and folly of expectation.*

◇ ◇ ◇

Hughbury Shamp is a teenager with one preoccupation: fame in Big Yolk, the city-solo. This keeps him sort of presexual, and that, it turns out, is the safest condition for one whose yearning puts him entirely at the mercy of more developed personalities. Shamp is also in effect parentless. He has his late father's railroad watch until Shipoff pinches it, and he recalls his mother when directly reminded:

> "Starboy, I'd like to do something for you. But I see by the bulge of your otherwise prepossessing eyeballs that your mother has hustled you out of consorting with strangers. Worn-out stump that she is, what does she know? Jawbones! There's no one else worth talking to."
>
> Now, a more misguided view of my mother's social legislation, hysterical purely on the incentive side, could hardly be imagined. But calling my mother a worn-out stump—I blinked. What a stroke! What second sight endowed him with this information?

All the same once Shipoff lures him off to Big Yolk, Shamp never gives his fleshly progenitors another thought. He has room only for his education. His masters each have *topoi*, as well as spiels which make these hypnotic—the Shipovian Calculus on the Recoil (S.C.O.R.), the World-Friar's introduction of the Waste Confession, Dr. Analarge's researches into the Inexpressible—but like everyone else in the city-solo these scholars have hidden programs and would hawk Shamp's flesh for a nickel to promote them.

If you stop seeing lives in terms of families and hometowns and judge by inner states instead, there was doubtless more affinity between Jaimy Gordon at 26 and Hughbury Shamp at 17 than one could admit back then. She had been deeply impressed by her education, almost entirely at the feet of, or by the texts of, men. She was wordstruck, adrift. Temporarily parentless, she had landed in a state of homeless hermithood between childhood and adulthood, which is more or less where Shamp ends up. *Shamp of the City-Solo* is a novel by a young woman who is sure of little except that she is word-ridden and, for worse as much as for better, one of a kind. At 26 I was certainly nothing but a writer, but somehow I wasn't coming out the recognizable article for the times. And to mark my distress over this I transported into Shamp's "Hindthoughts on His Own Magnificence" the passion of that other parentless compulsive blabber, miscellanist and lost-&-found soul Samuel Taylor Coleridge:

195

I had time out of mind given it up as a lost cause, given myself over, I mean, a predestined author, though without a drop of true author *blood in my veins.*

Likewise Hughbury Shamp, although he says *lector* instead of *author*. And likewise Jaimy Gordon. When some years later I began to see myself as more like other people, especially other women, than not like them, I began my second novel, *She Drove Without Stopping*.

A NOTE ON THIS EDITION

Shamp of the City-Solo was written between 1968 and 1973 in a series of partial drafts and two complete drafts; a copy of the first complete draft from the spring of 1972 can be found in the Brown University Library. The next complete draft, apparently lost, was made for the first published edition, which was issued in the spring of 1974 in a printing of 50 signed hardcover copies, approximately 950 paperback copies, and four specially bound copies *hors commerce*. That first edition, published by Treacle Press in Providence, Rhode Island, included twelve line drawings by James Aitchison; the titlepage was printed letterpress at Burning Deck Press and hand-tipped.

In 1980 Treacle Press issued a second edition in simultaneous hardcover and trade paperback bindings: all but one of the drawings were dropped; in addition, roughly one hundred corrections and additions were made by the author to the original setting of the text. Much of that edition was sequestered and destroyed in anticipation of the present one.

This third edition has been designed by Bruce McPherson and entirely reset in Linotronic Palatino. Alexandra Langley input and copyedited the typescript, basing the text on the second edition. Patricia Bruning set the text at Studio Graphics, Kingston, New York during the month of September 1993, incorporating additional corrections made by the author. Four of the original Aitchison drawings have been reinserted; the dustjacket features a fifth. A new drawing by Mr. Aitchison was also commissioned (pp. 100-101). The titlepage has been adapted from the cover to the second edition, as drawn by Paul Bacon. This edition has been printed and bound by McNaughton & Gunn Lithographers in Saline, Michigan.